I SIMPLY LOVEI _____ _____ TALES
collection from LOVESWEPT. As a dreamer and a
reader and a writer who grew up with Grimms'
fairy tales and an imagination that sometimes got
me into hot water, I envied my fellow LOVESWEPT
authors. What a golden opportunity they had not
only to revisit those wonderful stories but to retell
them from their own unique perspectives.

I read each book with admiration and awe—
and with a fervent wish to get a chance to tell my
own treasured tale someday. Well guess what? I
had to wait a year but it finally happened . . . and
I'm delighted to share this story with you.

The Prince and the Pauper was written by one
of America's best loved story tellers, Mark Twain.
It has sparked vivid fantasies for many of us.

When the hero of my book, Logan Prince,
encounters his double and decides to trade places,
he's looking for nothing more than a brief escape
from his life. Instead he finds a woman who
changes his cynical attitude about life . . . and
love.

This story is not only a celebration of the resili-
ence of the human spirit, but of the capacity for the
heart to heal, and to love. After all, that's what it's
all about, isn't it?

My very best wishes to you,

Cindy Gerard

WHAT ARE *LOVESWEPT* ROMANCES?

They are stories of true romance and touching emotion. We believe those two very important ingredients are constants in our highly sensual and very believable stories in the LOVESWEPT line. Our goal is to give you, the reader, stories of consistently high quality that may sometimes make you laugh, sometimes make you cry, but are always fresh and creative and contain many delightful surprises within their pages.

Most romance fans read an enormous number of books. Those they truly love, they keep. Others may be traded with friends and soon forgotten. We hope that each LOVESWEPT romance will be a treasure—a "keeper." We will always try to publish

LOVE STORIES YOU'LL NEVER FORGET
BY AUTHORS YOU'LL ALWAYS REMEMBER

The Editors

PERFECT DOUBLE

CINDY GERARD

BANTAM BOOKS

NEW YORK · TORONTO · LONDON · SYDNEY · AUCKLAND

PERFECT DOUBLE
A Bantam Book / January 1994

LOVESWEPT and the wave design are registered
trademarks of Bantam Books, a division of
Bantam Doubleday Dell Publishing Group, Inc.
Registered in U.S. Patent
and Trademark Office and elsewhere.

All rights reserved.
Copyright © 1993 by Cindy Gerard.
Cover photo copyright © 1993 by Mort Engel.
No part of this book may be reproduced or transmitted
in any form or by any means, electronic or mechanical,
including photocopying, recording, or by any
information storage and retrieval system, without
permission in writing from the publisher.
For information address: Bantam Books.

If you would be interested in receiving protective vinyl covers for your
Loveswept books, please write to this address for information:

Loveswept
Bantam Books
P.O. Box 985
Hicksville, NY 11802

ISBN 0-553-44300-3

Published simultaneously in the United States and Canada

PRINTED IN THE UNITED STATES OF AMERICA

OPM   0 9 8 7 6 5 4 3 2 1

To my dad
I miss you, Petey.

ONE

A half-drained tumbler of Scotch in hand, Logan Prince stared broodingly at the dazzling view of Houston at night. Thirty stories below, a flickering regiment of city lights and snaking traffic burned like a procession of guttering candles through a mist of July smog and humidity. The Prince-family money had bought him this view from the penthouse. As Preston Prince's son, he was born with the equivalent of Fort Knox for a bankroll and raised on such adages as "money breeds success, success breeds money." And power. Always power.

He shoved away from the window, then knocked back his glass and drained it. It was almost midnight. His stomach had turned to acid an hour ago as a persistent cliché clamped a stranglehold on his thoughts. It was lonely at the top.

Grimacing in self-disgust, he headed for the bar. "No points for originality there, Prince," he muttered, filling his glass with fresh ice. Tonight, it seemed, he wasn't up to thinking original thoughts. Truth was, he didn't want to think at all. What he wanted was out.

Now, there was a twist worth contemplating. Pensive, he covered the ice with Scotch. He wanted out, yet if the movers and shakers who were slack-jawed with the lust for power could read his mind, they'd be leaving footprints on each other's backs in the rush to squeeze in line for his position.

He tugged at the knot of his tie and stared at his drink, suddenly losing a taste even for that. Burnout. Wasn't that the term for what he was feeling? Burned out, tapped out, played out. And all this at the ripe old age of thirty-six.

He was exactly where he'd been groomed to be, where he'd worked like hell to get. He possessed the fortune he'd been born to and had subsequently doubled it in an effort to prove himself as the eventual successor to his father.

And there was the rub, wasn't it? The time had finally come. Preston Edward Prince, the reigning king of the castle, was about to step down as CEO of Prince Enterprises. And he, Logan James Prince, was set to inherit the proverbial corporate throne.

Lonely at the top. The line played like a needle stuck on a scratched LP. He worked his jaw, staring at the extravagant art collection displayed casually about the decorator showplace of a penthouse—and felt empty. The price of one piece, one single piece of the Peruvian pottery, could feed a family of five for a year. He was surrounded by opulence and wealth. He lived in a world of excess where everything was beautiful, coveted—sterile.

Yes, it was lonely at the top . . . and yet so crowded with regrets that he suddenly felt suffocated by lack of space.

Compelled by an urge so strong that he knew it would deal him a swift defeat if he fought it, he headed for the door. He had no idea where he was going. He knew only that he had to get out of there.

Ignoring the carefully concealed surprise of both the elevator operator and the doorman, he shouldered his way out onto the street. Humidity as thick and cloying as his regrets hit him full in the face. He shrugged out of his tuxedo jacket and tossed it along with his tie toward a nearby trash can.

And then he walked. Head down, fists jammed in his pockets, he walked. He walked fast and for a long time, not knowing or caring where he was going— until he felt the blunt, cold thrust of deadly steel shoved against his ribs from behind.

"Nice night for a stroll, eh? Oh, no, fancy man, you just keep walkin' and we won't get any blood on that prissy white shirt a yours." The voice was sandpaper gruff and edged with wild desperation. "And keep them hands right in those pockets so I know what they're doin'."

Logan did as he was told, glancing up and around him, realizing for the first time where his aimless wandering had taken him. It was not lovers' lane. It was the deepest and the meanest part of the city. And it was no place for a "fancy man."

"Take the wallet," he said, slowing his pace marginally so he could get a feel for the size of the man propelling him toward the dark opening of an alley a few yards ahead.

"Oh, I plan to. I'll have the wallet and a whole lot more. Me and the boys are figurin' on having some fun carving up that pretty-boy face a yours—right, boys?"

The "boys" materialized like rats out of the dank depths of the alley as Logan was pushed into the blackness.

He squared off against the faceless predators and the sharp click and flash of readied blades. There were four of them, each with an ax to grind against a society that made them gutter rats and made Logan the symbol of everything they'd never be.

He knew they meant to take him down, but it wouldn't be without a fight. "Sorry to disappoint you, gentlemen, but I'm afraid you didn't catch me in a party mood."

The chuckles were feral and confident in what they sensed was certain victory. Like a pack of wild dogs, they circled then lunged, crowding him into the midst of pounding fists and a kaleidoscope of sharp, ripping pain.

He got in several good licks before sheer numbers got the best of him. They beat him with studied relish—and then, suddenly, they stopped.

"Listen! I said listen, dammit!" the leader snarled, silencing the pack to a hush of labored breathing and muttered expletives. "Someone's coming."

They let Logan go. He dropped to all fours, spitting blood and fighting for consciousness, when he heard a shout. Hard-edged, streetwise, and commanding, it sent the rats scurrying after one final kick that hurled Logan face-first onto the cracked filth of the pavement.

The ringing silence that engulfed him was as welcome and eloquent as the absence of fists and steel-toed boots slamming into his ribs. It didn't last nearly long enough, though.

"Can you get up?"

He thought he could. He was wrong. The best he could manage was a groan.

"Look, man, I haven't ever been accused of being a guardian angel, I'm no hero, and I'm nobody's fool. They'll be back like flies shooed away from spilled beer. I don't really care how you do it, but you'd better get the hell up and get outta here."

Responding to the urgency in the voice, Logan tried again. Fire split like a whip crack through his ribs. He fell back to the concrete in a twisted heap.

Through a haze of exquisite agony, he heard a mumbled, "Why do I always let myself in for this kind of grief?" He gritted his teeth and fought to keep from passing out as he was hauled to his feet.

"Damn if we don't prove the rule," the same deep voice muttered, grunting against Logan's weight.

"There's a fool born every minute and we're two of the biggest. I'll haul your sorry self out of here, but I swear, if they come back and it comes down to saving your ass or mine, you're on your own."

"Fair"—the effort cost him but he finished— " . . . enough."

"Don't talk. Just walk. And I don't mean Sunday stroll."

Pain accompanied each newly discovered detail as Logan slowly came to. A creaking bed. Clean sheets. A neon sign blinking softly but steadily through a window into the dimly lit room. And a fragrance— sweet, fresh, floral—that became his motivation to claw an inch back toward consciousness.

The scent brought comfort, an oasis of relief in a desert of misery. It was a woman's scent, and with it came the caress of soft, soothing hands. He got lost in the feel of those hands. He wanted to stay lost . . .yet he wanted to see this woman whose hands made magic and whose scent would forever linger in his memory.

But when he managed to pry open his eyes and look at the wavering scowl on his angel's face, he was sure he was going to get another beating.

"You've got your nerve, Johnny Dallas." Her musical voice was completely at odds with her scolding tone as she carefully dabbed a cool cloth on his forehead. "Stumbling in here in the dead of night. Bloody and bruised as a damn alley cat. Don't you ever learn?

And don't you have someplace else to light every time you land your Anglo hide where it shouldn't ought to be?"

Logan hurt too much to question why this beautiful young woman seemed to think she knew him, or why she'd called him Johnny. Or to consider the contradictions of her stern, judgmental words pitted against her soft eyes and her gentle hands.

Her voice was soft too. Like her scent, it floated through the pain like a soothing balm as she worked over his beat-up face.

She was a very reluctant angel. But such a face this angel had. It was a Spanish face with a honey-warm complexion, huge dark eyes the color of hand-rubbed walnut, and a mouth that looked lush and ripe and molded for much more pleasurable endeavors than scowling.

He wanted to look at her forever. Wanting and accomplishing, however, were two entirely different things. Losing the battle to keep his eyes open, he had to settle for directing his dwindling energy toward assessing his condition instead.

A slow and cautious shifting told him his ribs were bandaged. The difficulty he was having breathing told him why. If a couple weren't broken, they were badly bruised.

"Don't move." She settled her hands gently but firmly on his shoulders before pressing another cool wet compress to his forehead.

He drifted with the sound of her voice and mouthed

a "Thank you," around the swollen flesh that used to be his lips.

She gave a very unladylike snort. "Save your thanks for someone who'll appreciate it."

Again she scolded. Again he formed the distinct impression that she was more concerned than angry.

He knew that unconsciousness would bring blissful oblivion. More than relief, though, he wanted another look at her. He forced his eyes open again, determined to hang on. The struggle was worth the effort.

She was a complete and utter contrast to the chic, elite women he was used to: Women who fluttered through his life like satin butterflies, cloaked in beauty but devoid of substance; women who needed their perfectly lacquered hair and designer clothes to conceal the scars they'd garnered while clawing their way up the social ladder.

He sensed that this woman, unlike them, had no such needs. No sharp edges. No predatory instincts. No ulterior motives. He could see it in her face. Feel it in her hands. She was the softest of women, a composite of every man's fantasy of what a woman should be. Unaffected. Pure. Sensual. Her expressive eyes shone with virginal innocence. Through them he could see a rich, rare heart.

And a shimmering sensuality.

He swallowed hard as she leaned in close. Another ache, this one heavy and low in his body, joined the others vying for attention.

She may have the face of a saint, but she had the body of a sinner. Her breasts were full and heavy, at once at odds yet in complete harmony with an earth-mother quality and a voluptuous siren's lure. Softly curved, lushly molded, her hips were a perfect complement to her tiny waist. He suspected he could span it with both hands. If he'd had the strength, he'd have reached for her and eliminated any doubt.

He must have groaned because she frowned. A wave of fatigue suddenly swamped him. Damning his weakness, he fought to keep her in focus. He didn't want to lose her and was certain he would if he let consciousness slip away.

Suspended somewhere between now and nowhere, and not wanting to give up on the now, he forced his eyes to remain open. Was she real? he wondered, searching her face. Or was she a wonderful fantasy his mind had manufactured to help combat his pain? Feeling a desperate need for an answer to his questions, he reached out to touch the thick, jet-black braid that fell over her left breast . . . and found substance and satin under his fingertips. Testing the heaviness of her hair in his hand, he brought the floral scent of it to his face and drew it in a silken caress across his lips.

"Just like you," she muttered in a hushed and husky attempt to sound angry. She tugged his hand away from her hair and set to work cleaning the cuts on his knuckles. "Stupid drunk and half-dead and you want to paw me. It's the only time you ever want me, though, isn't it, Johnny?"

Johnny. Why was she calling him Johnny? In some distant corner of his mind, he was angry that it was Johnny she thought she was taking care of. Whoever this Johnny was, he was a fool. Logan couldn't imagine any man, drunk or sober, not wanting this woman. Fire shot through his ribs, reminding him he was in no position to be calling anyone names.

Names . . . he didn't even know her name . . . or how he had ended up in her bed. Must be her bed, he thought, muzzily aware of pastel sheets, frilly pillows, and the rare flutter of a flouncy lace curtain stirred by a stingy hot breeze.

He felt himself going under and suddenly he was afraid he'd slip away without ever knowing who she was or if she was what she appeared to be. No woman he'd ever known had struck him as this genuine. He needed to know if she really was the exception.

He tried to ask her name. The words wouldn't come. He wet his lips and tried again. The only sound that came out was a long frustrated groan as he gave in to the black haze that enveloped him.

It was daylight. But for the ever-present company of the dismally familiar pain, Logan felt he was alone. Eyes closed, he tried to reconstruct a vague memory of having come to in this room, in this bed. Other memories, stronger ones, courted him. Gentle brown eyes and even gentler hands, a fragrance that was hauntingly elusive yet indelibly imprinted on his senses.

"So you're not dead after all. And just when I was beginning to suspect I'd have to find a place to dump the body."

Logan jerked his head toward the deep, male voice. Pain ricocheted inside his skull. When the haze cleared, he tried to focus on the man standing at the foot of the bed, and slowly the man's features became clear. For a moment all Logan could do was stare . . . and wonder if the beating he'd taken had affected his vision. Knowing what agony it would bring, he resisted the urge to shake his head. He closed his eyes instead and counted to a slow ten.

When he opened them again, nothing had changed. Standing in front of him was a man with eyes the same ice-blue color as his own. Eyes that could slice like a knife, or seduce with a look. His mouth—what Logan could see of it beneath a thick, chamois-colored mustache—was Logan's own mouth, thin and hard, one most people would characterize as cynical. Until he smiled. And when he smiled, as this man was doing now, it was the same smile that Logan had been told could charm the most ruthless of corporate moguls into mergers or lay the coldest of Houston's socialites between his sheets.

The resemblance didn't end there. His nose had the same sharp, clean lines and so did his strong, square jaw. Even his chin had the same deep cleft. And while the hair beneath a battered gray Stetson was longer and shaggier than his own, the color was the same tanned-leather blond.

Studying the man, Logan tried to make some sense of the phenomenon. At times during the night, he'd thought he might be dying. He'd even dreamed he'd seen an angel. Maybe he *had* died, because the man facing him now couldn't be from this world.

A sharp jab in his ribs assured him that he hurt too much to be dead. That meant that this cowboy, a mirror image of himself, was as real as his pain.

He watched in dazed silence as the man hooked his thumbs in his belt loops then slanted him a crooked grin.

"It's a kicker, ain't it?" the man asked in a heavy Texas drawl.

It was a kicker, all right. And if he hadn't already been flat on his back, Logan thought, the "kicker" would have knocked him there.

"Who the hell are you?" Logan's voice was a mere croak, his tongue was so swollen.

"Well, I ain't your long-lost twin, if that's what you had in mind."

But he could have been, Logan realized, finally accepting what he saw.

"Bit of a shock, huh? Meeting your double and you not even sure if you're afoot or on horseback."

Shock? As understatements went, that ranked with the biggest. Logan looked him over again. Aside from the face and the frame—and if everything else ran true to form, he stood a full six-two and carried the same one-ninety Logan weighed in at each morning—the voice, as well, had a familiar ring.

His memory suddenly caught hold. "It was you . . . you're the one who . . . called off the dogs last night."

"There ya go. No short-term memory loss. I'd say that's a good sign. The lump on your skull must not be as bad as it looks. The name's Dallas. Johnny Dallas. Don't bother to get up," he added with a sardonic quirk of his mouth.

Johnny Dallas. The name triggered another recent but elusive memory of the woman with soft brown eyes and even softer hands. He quickly scanned the room.

"She's not here," Dallas supplied when Logan's questioning gaze returned to his.

So his angel, whoever she was, had been real. He hadn't been dreaming. He felt a rush of relief before his heart started to beat faster. "She? Who is she? *Where* is she?"

"Her name is Carmen. She's at work."

"Carmen," he repeated, thinking how the name fit his memory of her—pretty, delicate, unique.

"Carmen Sanchez." Dallas hesitated then added meaningfully, "And she's a friend."

Logan swallowed and shifted, sucking in another harsh breath as his body reminded him of his stupidity with vicious relish. Another piece of memory clicked into place. His angel had called him Johnny. And as he lay there, staring at this man who said his name was Johnny Dallas, Logan realized why. "She . . . Carmen . . . she thinks I'm you."

Dallas grinned sheepishly. "Yeah, well, I couldn't stick around for intros or explanations last night. Besides, she was pulling a double shift at the hospital and wasn't supposed to come home until this afternoon. You were going to be gone before she ever saw you."

Logan tried to think that through. But it hurt to think. Hell, it hurt to breathe. A coma seemed a viable option. Silence would be a welcome relief.

Dallas, however, was in a talkative mood. "You wouldn't have lasted until dawn out on the street. I had to find a place to dump you, and Carmen's apartment was right around the corner," he continued, then scratched his jaw. "Only problem is, I figured I'd have you outta here before she got home and she'd never be the wiser. It wasn't until I came back to check on you a little before daylight and saw her leaving the apartment building that I realized she must have come home between shifts."

Logan frowned as more pieces of his memory sifted together. "She didn't seem particularly shocked to find a beat-up man in her bed."

"Not just a man," Dallas drawled. "She thinks you're me, remember? And she's patched me up before when the need arose."

He grimaced. "Happens often, does it?"

Another grin. "Often enough."

Logan squinted up at Dallas, wondering what other needs Carmen tended for him. His gut twisted with an emotion he didn't want to define as envy but would be hard-pressed to call by any other name. Lack of oxygen, he decided as he tried a deep breath, then checked it as a stabbing sensation shot through his ribs again.

"There's nothing for it, you know, but to haul out of that bed and get moving," Dallas said with a knowing chuckle. "You took your lumps, now you've got to live with 'em for a while. Coffee's hot in the kitchen. I figure if you can make it that far, you'll live to see tomorrow."

Logan glared at Dallas's back as the man whistled his way out of the bedroom. It wasn't bad enough that he was faced with a clone of himself—he had to listen to his Will Rogers philosophy as well.

Dallas was right, though. He had to start moving. Gingerly peeling back the covers, he gritted his teeth and inched to a sitting position. Fresh new tortures inspired by the activity wrung a groan from him. He'd been stripped to his boxers, he noticed before he limped to the kitchen.

Dallas was there with all the sympathy of a drill sergeant when Logan collapsed onto a chair, close to passing out again. Propping his scuffed cowboy boots on the table, Dallas shoved a steaming mug of coffee under Logan's nose.

The smell of the coffee helped. It would help even more if he could drink it. Discounting the fact that he hadn't yet regained the strength to lift the mug to his mouth, the thought of what the steaming hot liquid would feel like on his battered lips gave him the patience to wait until it cooled off.

Dallas, who had been studying him speculatively, shifted his hips, dug into his pocket, and pulled out a wallet. "Found it this morning near a trash can." He tossed it on the table. "Figured, from the ID, it must be yours. Figured from the address you'd never *heard* of this end of town, let alone come a-callin'."

In spite of Dallas's good-ol'-boy drawl and complete lack of hostility, the uncanny resemblance to himself still set Logan on edge. It was like looking in a mirror with a mind of its own—and an attitude.

"Spooky, ain't it?" Dallas asked, picking up Logan's wallet and studying the picture ID. "Put you in a mustache or shave off mine and there's not a dime's worth of difference between us. Unless, of course, you start comparing bankrolls. Then I suspect the differences would mount up real soon."

Logan eyed him speculatively. So Dallas knew who he was. Not that he was surprised. The Prince name had been high profile in Texas for decades. "It would seem that I owe you."

Dallas grunted. "You owe lady luck. She just put me in the right place at the right time. Don't get any notion that I played hero. If your friends hadn't lit out of there first thing out of the blocks, I'd have been long gone, and you'd have been vulture meat this morning—not that you look much better than that right now. Lord, if you aren't one sorry-lookin' son of a gun." He chuckled, shaking his head sympathetically.

"Bankroll or no, man, it would take a hell of a deal to make me want to trade places with your headache today."

"Trade places? Now there's an idea that has possibilities," Logan said glumly. "At this very moment I'd gladly pay any price to be free of this bitching pain.

"I could make it worth your while," he added, taking a feeble stab at prolonging the joke. "Name your price. What would it take to put you in my shoes?"

Dallas gave a sage snort over the rim of his coffee cup. "Tell you what, you take two aspirin and call me in the morning. If you're still of a mind to talk trade, I'll consider it then."

Wishing it were that easy, Logan tried for a smile, which he quickly curbed when his split lip protested.

Trading places. The notion snagged in his thoughts for another moment, holding far too much appeal. And in that moment before he dismissed it as pure nonsense, it settled, big as life and twice as compelling.

"You know"—Dallas's voice was pensive, considering—"most people showing their face in the district that time of night are either looking to score, looking for trouble, or not looking at all. I figure I know which category you fall into. Only question now is why."

Why? Logan propped his elbows on the table and gingerly lowered his head to his hands. Because he'd been running, that's why. Because he'd been looking for a way out and not looking where he was going. Because he'd been so desperate for a break in the action, he'd stumbled into hostile territory. He'd made a near-fatal tactical error all because he'd wanted a reprieve.

He still did, in spite of the beating he'd taken. His head came up when he realized how much he still did. He stared at Dallas with renewed interest. And in that moment, that crystalline, crisp, all-senses-on-overload moment, he realized he not only wanted the reprieve but the means to that end was sitting across the table, staring him in the face.

He eyed Dallas thoughtfully. It was ridiculous, of course, the idea of trading places. Ridiculous. But that didn't mean it couldn't work.

He gave Dallas a longer, more critical look and recognized some subtle differences that would distinguish one man from the other. The blue of Dallas's eyes was a shade grayer than his own; Dallas's hair, a sun streak lighter. He was built more on the slim side, too, with a cowboy leanness acquired from manual labor as opposed to the more sculpted body Logan had honed and molded in an exclusive Houston health club.

Still, even considering the differences, the resemblance *was* remarkable. Get rid of Dallas's mustache, smooth out his rough edges, and it would take a very discriminating eye to tell them apart. And now that he was over the shock of confronting a man who was so close to his exact double, the prophetic implication of their chance meeting was undeniable.

They actually could trade places and no one would be the wiser. In fact, Carmen Sanchez, who evidently knew Dallas well, had already been fooled. Granted, his face looked like minced meat, but he'd still resembled Dallas enough that she hadn't questioned who he was.

He should be questioning, though, and highly suspect of his reasoning powers. A man in full control of his faculties would not be seriously considering what under ordinary circumstances would have been a totally ludicrous proposition.

But these weren't ordinary circumstances, were they? And the fact was, Dallas was the solution he'd been looking for. His way out . . . albeit a temporary one.

All he needed was a month. One month of anonymity. One month of time out from the crush of Prince Enterprises' expectations. One month of reprieve before he took over the helm and wouldn't be heard from again outside a corporate boardroom.

And in the back of his mind was the niggling notion that trading places with Dallas would provide something else—an opportunity to see Carmen Sanchez again. To see if reality measured up to the memory of his reluctant angel. To see if she could possibly be as uniquely genuine as he'd sensed she was. To see if a woman would think of him with something other than dollar signs and social position on her mind.

Where the hell had that come from? He wasn't looking for romance. He wasn't even looking for sex. Sex was a commodity that had been his for the asking as soon as the lady had sniffed out his pedigree.

He shook off the cynicism provoked by that knowledge and stared at Dallas again. It could work. And what could happen in a month? What did he really have to lose pitted against what he stood to gain?

His mind raced to explore the possible repercussions. It wasn't as if Dallas would be calling any shots. He'd let Ben in on the switch. Ben Crenshaw had been Logan's right-hand man for ten solid years. If push came to shove, Ben could handle just about anything that came up in his absence anyway.

The conclusion became increasingly obvious. And the plan he was formulating gained more merit by the second. Dallas had been dropped in Logan's lap. He'd be a fool not to take advantage. All he had to do was get Dallas to agree to the bluff.

His decision made, he fell back on the knowledge that if there was one thing he'd mastered in his career, it was the ability to manipulate people.

"So, Dallas," he began, before he could talk himself out of it. "What piece of blue Texas sky would it take to lure you into considering a business proposition?"

TWO

It had been remarkably easy, really. From the formulation of the plan to the sealing of the deal, everything had gone smoothly. Dallas had his eye on a little ranch near San Antonio. If he fulfilled his part of the bargain, he would get a loan from Logan to secure the property and enough working capital to get off to a running start. A lengthy phone call to Ben, who, although skeptical, finally agreed to go along with the charade like the loyal employee Logan knew he was, set the wheels in motion. By noon, when Ben arrived to pick up Dallas, everything was in place, and Logan felt confident Ben would cover all the fine points along the way.

Sputtering orders to Logan to get himself to a doctor, Ben left with Dallas in tow, assuring Logan he'd stick to him like needles on a cactus. One of the things that made Ben so valuable was his expertise at evasion: He would keep Dallas just out of everyone's reach and everyone's eye as much as possible. Yes,

Ben was a master at dodging suspicions before they even materialized. If need be, he'd plead laryngitis and the need to rest the voice to avoid questions about Dallas's good-ol'-boy drawl. Dallas was more than willing to cooperate. The only fuss he made was over the loss of his mustache and the need for a haircut—and even that was good-natured.

For a long time after they'd left, Logan lay on the bed and stared at the ceiling. If he could have moved, he supposed now would be the time to jump for joy— or the well-bred, socially acceptable equivalent thereof. His spontaneity had been suppressed for too long, however, behind layers of staunch control aimed at the appearance of glacial indifference. He wasn't sure how to react . . . or even if he was *capable* of an honest reaction. And, he suspected, that was really what this was all about.

He was a lucky man. He knew that. He possessed the wealth and position most men envied. But he needed to get grounded again. He needed to find out who Logan Prince was when he wasn't cutting deals and calling shots. He needed to know if there was more to the man than the business machine.

He supposed he should be feeling a little panic, or even a spark of elation that he was actually getting this opportunity. Instead he felt a numb sort of peace.

Alone, exhausted from the mental effort to absorb all the personal data Dallas had thrown at him and from the disgustingly minimal exertion of pulling on a pair of Dallas's jeans, he focused on combating his physical pain. It was more than a nuisance. It was the one thing of substance over which he couldn't seem to gain the upper hand.

Then he thought of Carmen Sanchez—and substance took on a whole new dimension. Suddenly he didn't feel numb anymore.

He told himself it was only a physical response. Male reacting to female. Nothing more. Simple. Natural. Biological.

He tried to dismiss his reactions, yet impressions of dark eyes and soft hands wove and blended sweetly as he drifted into a restless sleep, wondering when she'd return and he could see her again, wondering why nothing had penetrated his armor of indifference for years and now merely thinking of her set all his senses humming.

Carmen Sanchez was not what this time-out was about, he reminded himself. It shouldn't be so difficult to remember. It shouldn't be, but somehow it was.

Long shadows were playing across the floor by the time the click of a key in a lock woke him. From the dusky darkness of her bedroom, from the intimacy of her bed, he listened to her moving about the apartment. To the rustle of grocery sacks. To the opening and closing of the refrigerator door. To her sigh of fatigue from a long day.

To the escalating beat of his heart.

She was tired. He fought a totally foreign twinge of remorse that she still had him to contend with.

She'd pulled a double shift, Dallas had said, before filling him in with a quick yet thorough rundown on his sullen angel.

Angel, it seemed, was the term that best described her. According to Dallas, if a lost child needed tending, if a foolish man needed mending, Carmen was there to carry the load. She was an Emergency Room nurse at Ben Taub Trauma Center. And when she had any spare time, she spent it doing volunteer work at Casa de Amigos Community Health Center.

That would explain the tidy job she'd done patching him up. It would also afford him the solitude he needed to see this through. Even if he stayed in her apartment for the duration, their paths rarely would cross once he was on his feet again. The woman, it seemed, worked twenty-four hours a day. He thought grimly that their workaholic tendencies might be the only thing they had in common.

In all other aspects, they were worlds apart. Money, education, social status, cultural heritage were the lines of demarcation drawn through time without their input or awareness.

As Dallas had so aptly put it, Logan had never "come a-callin" in this part of town before. And on his brief and unsteady sojourn from the bedroom to the kitchen and back to the bedroom again, he'd caught glancing impressions of how modestly she lived.

According to Dallas, she shared this two-bedroom apartment with her brother, Rico, who was currently midway through a three-month shift on a Gulf oil rig. Dallas was a friend of Rico's and had the dubious responsibility of looking out for Carmen in her brother's absence.

From everything Logan had gathered, Dallas was the one who needed looking after. He was a goodhearted drifter, down on his luck, short on cash, even shorter on common sense. Between women, he shared Carmen's extra bedroom with Rico.

Dallas had made it clear that his interest in Carmen was strictly fraternal. Though Logan's memory of last night was a bit hazy, he remembered seeing something in her eyes and hearing something in her voice as she'd alternately scolded and soothed him while tending to his injuries that made him suspect her feelings for Dallas ran deeper. For some reason he didn't want to explore, that thought didn't settle well.

Soft footsteps sounded in the hallway, bringing him back to the present. A fragrance drifted into the room. He wasn't hazy where that fresh, delicate scent was concerned. He'd recognize it anywhere.

He turned his head, much too eager, much too pleased to see her standing hesitantly in the doorway. A swift and explosive excitement surged through his blood as he looked at her. A profound and deep sense of contentment followed when she moved to his side.

Too stunned by his reactions to fight them, he let them have free rein. He indulged a need to simply watch her.

He searched her eyes, somehow not surprised to find them as soft and as telling as he remembered. A man could get lost in those eyes, in the undisguised caring, in the dark, liquid warmth. He remembered getting lost in them last night. Those eyes spoke for her . . . of longing, quite possibly of love, of a pride that wouldn't let her confess aloud what she thought her silence protected.

It protected nothing. He could see it all too clearly. She cared about Dallas; she was as obvious and as vulnerable to attack as a fledgling business was to a corporate takeover.

Like a physical touch, electric, sensual, soul mending, she projected her feelings with each hesitant caress of her gaze. He felt an unsolicited sting of regret knowing she was looking at him and thinking he was Dallas. On its heels came a swift, explosive anger, another emotion he rarely allowed himself to indulge.

Dallas was a fool, he decided, and thought it pathetically sad that he, a stranger to this woman, could so easily see what Dallas either refused to acknowledge or simply didn't care to recognize.

And he would be a bigger fool than Dallas, he told himself, if he didn't back away from this encroaching temptation to experience everything her eyes promised. In the first place, the love she offered wasn't for him. In the second, he knew love was an illusion. He'd learned that particular lesson early on.

It wasn't that he was bitter. He was realistic. Women loved the idea of his money. He didn't fault them for it. Money, after all, was the great motivator. He understood its lure. But he also understood that the concept of "love" was nothing more than a time-honored deception. He was wise enough not to buy into it.

He watched Carmen Sanchez's face as she carefully and skillfully examined his bandaged ribs, and he decided that she had not yet learned that valuable lesson. Her gentle expression told him she was still a believer. He didn't know whether to pity her or envy her. And watching her, he found himself wishing he weren't so wise—or so jaded.

"You need to see a doctor." Her voice was thick with concern and caring.

He managed a subtle shake of his head. "You." He swallowed back the dryness of his throat. "I only need you."

The words surprised him. That they were true surprised him even more. He did need her. He needed the openness she projected, but that she wasn't aware was so special. He needed the compassion she gave, but that he hadn't been aware was a necessity.

She was visibly unsettled. Her hands were shaking as she gently supported his head and brought a glass of water to his lips. "Here. Drink. Just a little."

The water felt cool going down and almost as good as the nestling warmth of her body, so close to his.

Too soon, her hand and her warmth were gone.

Her eyes were suspiciously moist and glistening when she eased away. "Who did this to you?"

"Doesn't matter," he croaked, aware of a dawning realization that emotions he hadn't ever claimed he owned were making themselves known with a flurry of activity. "It's not as bad as it looks," he added quickly, trying to deny a wave of protectiveness prompted by the pain in her expression.

"Oh, and now you know more about medicine than I do? You're lucky they didn't beat you to death." Fire and fury peppered her words and brightened her eyes, along with a telling tear.

"When are you going to grow up, Johnny? When are you going to learn? As long as Carmen is here to patch you up, you think you can play your macho games just for the fun of it, don't you? Have you forgotten so soon that Rico was almost killed?"

It was glaringly obvious that seeing him like this—seeing *Dallas* like this—hurt her. Try as he might to deny it, Logan felt jealously ripple through him like a hot Houston wind.

The fact that she was hurting affected him far more than his wounded pride—or his inability to catalog and file away all the unexpected feelings she kept managing to draw out of him. He was moved by her pain. And he wanted to do something to minimize it. To that end, he didn't stop to think about the wisdom of touching her, he simply did it.

Cupping her face in his palm, he brushed his thumb over the hot, heavy tear tracking down her cheek. Her skin was so delicate. And he realized, so were her feelings.

He was completely out of his element. He didn't know how to handle what was happening to her. For that matter, he didn't know how to handle what was happening to him.

Ask anyone who knew him and they'd tell you that Logan Prince didn't have a heart. He'd traded it in long ago for the price of a corporate kingdom. Liquid silver, not blood, ran through his veins. Silver readily convertible to cash. Callous and cold as that assessment was, he'd always accepted it as accurate.

So he didn't have a clue as to why her pain was affecting him. Or why a lump the size of Texas formed in his throat when he tried to swallow back a surge of sympathy he wasn't supposed to be capable of feeling.

Abruptly he let his hand fall away, determined to stay true to his reputation. It was more difficult than he'd anticipated.

"I'm sorry if I've upset you," he heard himself whisper.

"You're sorry." She sniffed, attempting a brave, huffy front. "Today you're sorry, sorry that your body is one big raw nerve. But you'll forget the pain soon enough, and the next time you get a notion to pick a fight, you'll drag your *sorry* self back to me."

She turned to go. With supreme effort he reached out and snagged her wrist.

"I am sorry," he insisted, compelled by an inexplicable need to assure her that it was not his intent to cause her pain—and suspecting that before he left her, he probably would.

"Save your sorrys, Johnny. But don't expect me to patch you up again, okay? I can't stand to see someone I care about hurting like this." She blinked hard. "I'll get you something to eat."

His grip on her wrist tightened in response to the resignation darkening her eyes.

She stood, looking everywhere except at him. But he saw it all, everything she didn't want him to see. The fatigue in her eyes was evident, and the feelings in her heart as well.

Carmen Sanchez would never make it in a boardroom. She never would be able to pull off a bluff. Neither would she take advantage of her sexuality to strike a bargain in a bedroom. It would never occur to her to try; even if she did, her emotions would give her away. She wore them like her fragrance. Sweetly. Without guile. Honestly. Without pretense.

And that, he realized, was what was giving him so much trouble. He was unaccustomed to such honesty. He'd had little experience handling it. If he was as jaded as he was accused of being, then why was he so affected by her pride? Why was he affected by her at all?

Look at her. Even now, the truth preempted her resolve to be angry. While her mouth was set in a grim, hard line, her eyes, her soft Spanish eyes, betrayed how much she cared.

He let go of her wrist, telling himself he couldn't afford to become entangled with her emotions or his. He was here only to bide time.

Yet when she turned in silence and left the room, he suspected that this great deception of his could have set something bigger in motion. And for a long time after she left the bedroom, he lay there pitting an escalating desire to take everything she was offering Dallas, against the most damnable urge to protect her from himself.

A sixth sense warned Carmen something was wrong. She spun away from the stove to see Johnny teetering in the doorway. Racing across the room, she reached him as he stumbled. She caught him as he was about to go down.

"What are you doing out of bed?" She eased his arm over her shoulder and took his weight. "Crazy Anglo. You want to keel over from lack of strength and crack another rib?"

As a nurse, she knew that while his injuries were seriousness, they weren't life threatening—*if* he gave himself time to heal.

As a woman, however, she empathized with his pain and the beating to his pride as he had to hang on and let her walk him the rest of the way to the kitchen table.

"I'm fine," he murmured weakly.

"You're fine. And I'm Mary, Queen of Scots," she said. His face was as white as her uniform. She suspected it took every ounce of his will to keep from passing out as she helped him into a kitchen chair.

Her arm was still around him when he looked up and into her eyes. A mere inch or two away, his blue gaze searched her face with a startling intensity.

She'd always thought of blue as cool. Until Johnny. The blue of his eyes was like the dazzling center of a dancing flame, fluid heat, liquid fire. The touch of his bare skin burning through her clothes and searing almost painfully against her breast was the only heat that even came close.

In that moment, with their gazes and bodies locked, she felt a sharp awareness of herself as a woman.

"You shouldn't be up," she said breathlessly, telling herself the intense physical contact was the reason she thought she saw that something in his eyes she sometimes fantasized about seeing. "You should have called me. What were you thinking, getting up by yourself?"

"That I missed you." His voice was gruff with pain and fatigue, his eyes smoky with all the longing any woman could ever hope for.

She lowered her lashes and looked away. Slowly, carefully, she eased away from his side. When she was certain he was steady, she walked back to the counter. Less than steady herself, she was acutely aware that he was watching her.

In silence, in confusion, she tossed her braid over her shoulder and went back to preparing his supper.

She'd known Johnny for a little less than three months now. In that time he'd never looked at her the way he was looking at her now: The way a man looks at a woman when he wants her. The way a man could look in order to make a woman feel hot on the inside, shivery cold on the outside, wistful and wanton everywhere in between.

Shaken by that look, she told herself she was imagining it. A man didn't change overnight. A man like Johnny would never change.

Sorry fool that she was, she'd fallen half in love with Johnny Dallas on first sight. Bad, sad seed that he was, she hadn't been able to help herself. In spite of his lack of ambition and his roving eye, he had a kind and generous heart, a teasing, flirty light in his eyes, and enough dazzle to charm the sun from the blue Texas sky.

She was a sucker for a killer smile and a man in need of a good woman to straighten him out. Sometimes she even thought she wanted to be that woman for Johnny. She thought of those times as her "sanity lapses." Unfortunately she had them a little too often around Johnny. On the flip side, a swift dose of common sense never failed to turn her around. She was determined to avoid what her friend Barb cataloged as every woman's once-in-a-lifetime shot at falling for exactly the wrong man. She wasn't about to let herself in for that kind of heartache.

Besides, Johnny liked his life the way it was: Short on commitment and long on wild women. She was light-years away from either, and wasn't willing to compromise. Not even for him.

While her heart had tumbled like a toddler venturing that first shaky step, she'd known straightaway that she was lucky he'd never been able to see her as anything but Rico's kid sister.

That knowledge didn't stop her from wishing for a little romance, though. As always, she kept it to herself.

"Smells good," he said gruffly, breaking into her thoughts.

She glanced over her shoulder at him, wondering at the raspy quality of his voice, worrying if one of the blows he'd taken had damaged his vocal cords. He didn't sound like himself. Didn't act like himself either. And she was beginning to think she was not mistaken about the way he was looking at her. It was intimate, that look. Full of longing and wonder and studied speculation.

He's hurting, she reminded herself. How do you expect him to act? She turned back to the saucepan on the front burner. "I made you some soup. Hopefully you can get it down without too much difficulty."

Silence settled again, uncomfortable, crowded with that electric, expectant edge she couldn't seem to ignore. Maybe the shock of finding him so badly beaten had prompted this undercurrent of sexual tension. Maybe it was seeing him in her bed.

Seeing him in her bed. Heat flared in her cheeks. Beaten and bloody, he was still some kind of dangerous-looking Anglo. All six-plus bare feet of him. Even now, dressed in a pair of faded denims, she couldn't rid herself of the picture of his long, muscled self sprawled out across her sheets.

Not that she hadn't seen her share of naked men. She was a nurse. It came with the territory. But she *hadn't* seen her share of naked men in *her* bed. And while she'd admit to spending a few lonely nights wondering how Johnny would look lying there, the reality far outshone the fantasy.

Would you listen to yourself, Sanchez? The man is in a bad way and you're thinking about physical activities that would have stressed Don Juan in his heyday. What is the problem here?

The problem, she finally decided, was that he seemed different. Something about him—not just the way he looked at her, not just the fact that he was hurt—was so very different. The difference finally came to her.

She spun around and took a long look at his face. "When did you shave off your mustache?"

Several tightly strung moments passed before he answered.

"I don't know. Couple of days ago, maybe."

She allowed herself a long, hungry look at his mouth. His poor, battered mouth. A mouth she'd never seen as clearly as she'd have liked, hidden as it was beneath his mustache.

She could see it now. Even swollen and bruised, it was quite glorious. She stared at his lips and knew why he had no shortage of lovers who would be willing to do all those sweet sultry things a woman could do to take her man's mind off his pain.

Her reaction was involuntary. She licked her own lips, then drew her lower one between her teeth before raising her gaze to his—and discovered he'd caught her staring.

She quickly lowered her lashes, but not before she'd caught sight of a dangerous and tummy-tightening darkness that shadowed his eyes.

"I . . . think I . . . like it," she stammered. " . . . the mustache. That you shaved it off, I mean. The haircut too. Of course, it's a little hard to tell, given the condition of your face."

He slowly raised a hand and explored the face in question. "Feels better already."

"Sure it does." Her gentle smile told him how much credence she gave his remark. Nothing on his body could possibly feel better. It would be a few days, in fact, before he'd be able to make that claim in earnest.

He was such a fraud. Such a tough, macho fraud. And he was such a contradiction. So was she. All this time she'd wondered if he would ever look at her like this, and now too much heat, too much attention, had her wringing the nap out of a hand towel.

A hot sweet affair did not fit into her plans. And while an affair with Johnny would definitely be hot and sweet, it would also be short. She wanted nothing short of long-term, or she wanted nothing at all.

She quickly went to the counter, still at a loss

to understand what was happening between them, but determined not to entertain any more thoughts about it.

"What about your job, Johnny?" she asked, needing a diversion. "You can't go to work. Not in your condition. But if you don't show up, won't they fire you?"

He was silent for a long moment. "It was a lousy job. I'll find another one."

Typical Johnny Dallas reaction. She didn't have to look at him to know he had that "I don't give a damn" look on his face. She shook her head sadly. "Easy come, easy go, right?"

He had to have heard what she couldn't hide. Disgust and regret. His lack of drive and inability to commit were his own business. He was a walk-away Joe and she knew he was doing her a favor by not giving her the time of day.

"Why do you put up with me, Carmen?" he asked softly, as if reading her mind.

Despite her determination not to react, something in the way he said her name made her go all soft again inside. "I don't," she said in a quiet voice. "I put up with Rico—*he* puts up with you."

"Why is that, do you suppose?"

Gruff with fatigue and pain, his voice made her shiver with an unexpected longing to feel his whispery words feather across her skin. She shrugged to hide her reaction. "As if you didn't know."

"Humor me. I'm wounded."

She cast him a puzzled look. He forced a quick,

lopsided grin—one that caused him pain. One that caused her heartbeats to stumble over each other in crazy, clumsy thuds.

She gazed at the counter, praying she didn't lop off a finger chopping vegetables for a salad, as she chastised herself under her breath in rapid-fire Spanish.

"I didn't catch that."

"You weren't supposed to."

"Talk to me, Carmen. It helps take the edge off."

She drew a deep breath, knowing she couldn't deny him. "Rico puts up with you because you saved his foolish hide and you know it," she said stiffly.

"And I've taken advantage of your hospitality ever since, haven't I? Why do you let me do that?"

Why? The stray-dog syndrome, she supposed. Couldn't turn one away. Now was the time to change that dirty shirt, if there ever was one. If she had a gram of common sense, she'd agree with him and tell him it was time to hit the road. Tell him she was tired of him showing up on her doorstep and camping out whenever he damn well pleased—or when he'd had a tiff with one of his women and she'd told him to take the closest door marked EXIT.

But she wasn't smart enough to tell him that. And what good would it do anyway? She suspected she would never be completely free of him, no matter where he was. Better off, no doubt, but never free.

Above it all, though, she felt she owed him. "In your own way, I think you've helped straighten Rico out."

That was the truth. Johnny might lack ambition, but his heart was usually in the right place. He'd talked to Rico. And Rico had listened. She couldn't help but have a soft spot for Johnny because of that.

"In the three months since you dragged him home beaten half to death, he's gotten himself together." She stared without seeing for a moment, lost in remembered fear for her brother. "He looked even worse than you do now. I was afraid for a while I'd lose him." She shivered, then pulled herself together. "But it's over now. He's doing fine."

"He doesn't talk about it much," she heard him say hesitantly before adding, "Who was it, do you think? Who beat him so badly?"

She went back to the stove to stir the soup. She wondered if the blows to his head could have caused some short-term memory loss. She didn't think so. Still, she decided to watch him closely over the next few days for signs of trouble. In the meantime she decided to do as he asked and humor him.

"Rico doesn't talk to me about it either. But I know who was responsible. Loan sharks had him tied in so tight he couldn't meet their payments. The beating was a warning." Another involuntary shiver rippled through her as she crossed the small kitchen. "Thank God they didn't kill him. And thank God they've left him alone since."

Her heart lurched to her throat as a horrible thought suddenly struck her. Her knife clattered to the counter, punctuating her fear. "Oh, Johnny, the men who beat you, were they . . . ? After what they did to Rico, tell me you weren't stupid enough to get into them for money too!"

"No, Carmen," he quickly assured her. "I was mugged. It's that simple. And that stupid. I wasn't watching my back."

Relief was swift and unsteadying. Her shoulders sagged, and she sank against the counter. When she met his gaze again, however, it was narrowed with edgy concern.

"Carmen . . ." he began, his scowl dark and ominous, "if Rico couldn't meet the payments, why have they left him alone since then?"

She dropped her chin against her chest. Men were insensitive, unappreciative dolts, all of them. And *this* man was blind as well. And stupid, she added in disgust. She worked double shifts. She'd sold all of her good furniture and replaced it with the bare essentials. She lived the Spartan existence of a nun. And he had to ask why the sharks weren't bothering Rico?

The bleak look in her eyes must have given him his answer. He glanced quickly around the modest apartment. She had to make better than a living wage on an RN's salary, but everything in the apartment suggested she was living from hand to mouth.

"You paid them off, didn't you?"

"Of course I paid them off. What else could I do? He's my brother."

"As if that explains everything."

"Yes," she said softly and without hesitation.

He studied her as if trying to understand what she was all about. "Loyalty. It means everything to you, doesn't it?" he asked finally.

She didn't answer.

"You're so loyal you practically impoverished yourself for your brother."

She listened for judgment in his words, listened for a note that implied she was a fool. What she heard instead was a quiet, sincere admiration. Coming from Johnny, who threw caution to the wind, and who professed to look out only for himself, but in practice did just the opposite, it was a rare and stunning compliment.

That didn't mean she thought what she'd done was anything extraordinary.

"I wanted him out from under their control. I'd have done whatever it took to make sure he was free of them."

"Whatever?" he asked darkly.

She turned back to the sink, shaken by the look in his eyes that relayed anger and concern in equal measures.

"He doesn't deserve you, Carmen."

She didn't see it that way at all. And she didn't understand his reactions.

"What you have to realize about Rico is that he's always had this strong need to prove himself. He measures his worth by his possessions. It's wrong, I know. But we grew up poor, Johnny. Like you. You should be able to identify with that. And you should be able to understand how he could get involved with those men."

Yeah, right, Logan thought cynically. Identify? Not quite. Understand? Hardly. Regardless of the wealth he'd taken for granted all his life, he couldn't quite see himself taking advantage of a woman the way Rico had taken advantage of Carmen. He hoped for her sake she was right about Rico straightening out. He hoped so for Rico's sake, too, because if he ever found out that her brother had a lapse and went back to using her, he'd personally see to it he'd never make that mistake again.

Oh, this is great, he thought in disgust. Will you listen to yourself? You've got no responsibility here. You've got no ownership. And you've got no right to judge. You plan to use her too.

The truth of his last thought echoed like a gunshot.

He *did* plan to use her. No matter how he colored it, he realized he had been thinking about doing so from the first moment he'd seen her.

It was so clear now. He'd orchestrated this bluff on the pretense of being burned out on corporate games and boardroom politics. While all that was true, she was the real reason he'd carried it through. One look from this woman whose eyes offered so much and whose body promised unlimited pleasure and he'd wanted her. Pared down, it was that basic. Pared down, it was that intense.

He was playing out this charade because of her.

Because of the way she'd looked at him during that first misty encounter when he'd awakened in her bed. He'd recognized even then what she could give him. Something special. Something real. Something rare.

For the first time in his life he was in a position to experience pure emotion. Simple truths. Unaffected feelings that weren't colored or covering ulterior motives.

She didn't know who he was. In fact, she thought he was someone else. What would it feel like, he wondered, to know a woman wanted him not because of who he was, but because of who he wasn't? As Johnny Dallas, he wasn't a rich man. He was only a man. As Johnny Dallas, he wasn't the "social and financial catch of the decade." He was only a man.

Only a man. He'd never been only a man before. He'd never wanted to be. He'd always been *the* man. *The* man to watch out for. *The* man to impress. *The* man to contend with. And he'd gladly risen to every role.

For this brief window in time, however, the opportunity to be something less—or something much more—was disarmingly appealing.

The irony of his thoughts should have made him laugh. It didn't. And the fact that it didn't told him he was treading on dangerous ground.

He looked at the woman who was, in essence, responsible for perpetuating that danger . . . Which of them, he wondered, stood the biggest chance of coming out of this unharmed?

THREE

Logan slowly became aware that Carmen was watching him. Concern darkened her eyes to ebony, as if she, too, recognized a clear and present danger. She should be concerned, he thought grimly. And he was only kidding himself if he thought she wouldn't be the one who got hurt if he played this through.

He clenched his hands into tight, tense fists as the depth of his intended deception sobered him. He might have earned his reputation for being ruthless, but he also had gained respect from his peers for his honesty. Yet he'd compromised that honesty the moment he'd started this switch. He'd crossed the line.

And as he watched her with increasing awareness of her vulnerability, he realized he'd be delving into other unknown territory if he hurt her. Guilt had never come to play in Logan Prince's domain. His father had taught him long ago that there was no room for guilt in business or life. Some people were users. Some people got used. It was part and parcel of the overall scheme of things, a natural order and balance to power. Those Midas rules were the foundation for his father's edicts. Those rules were absolutes and constants.

Logan tried to anchor himself in those constants. Then he looked at Carmen—and he knew something was happening to him that threatened to rip that anchor from its mooring.

Desperately he worked to convince himself that whatever happened between them was destined to happen. If she got hurt, it would be her fault, not his—and it would be her fault, too, if her sense of self-worth was diminished by the time he left her. She was an adult. He wasn't responsible for her actions or reactions.

When she moved to his side and placed that wonderfully cool hand on his forehead, however, he suspected it was his reactions he should be worrying about.

The woman did extraordinary things to him. The longer he was around her, the more difficult it was to see things in black and white. With one look, she could have him second-guessing his priorities. With one look she could crumble stone to dust.

He swallowed hard, thinking of touching her . . . her flesh soft and giving, and he steeled himself against an illicit need to have her.

"Are you all right?" she asked, mistaking his apparent turmoil for pain.

"I'm fine," he managed to say in a gritty whisper.

She frowned. "I think you've been up too long. You don't even sound like yourself." When he didn't respond, she prompted, "Johnny?"

He made a mistake then. He let himself be moved by the concern showing on her face. As much as he wanted her, he didn't like the idea of hurting her. For a man who had always taken what he wanted, the prospect of self-denial was as painful as his battered ribs.

Lowering his head to his hands, he swore under his breath.

"You're in pain, aren't you?"

"Would you quit worrying about me and take care of yourself?" It came out as a growl, like the snarling warning of an animal boxed into a corner. Any animal would attack if pushed hard enough. He suddenly felt he'd been pushed to the limit.

"That's it. I'm helping you back to bed."

"No," he insisted darkly. No matter how rough he felt, he didn't want to be anywhere near her or her bed at the moment. He needed some distance from her. Trouble was, he didn't think he was capable of moving. "You haven't even taken time to change out of your work clothes. Go change. I'll be fine."

She stood at his side for a moment, hesitant to leave him alone.

Didn't the woman have a shred of instinct when

it came to self-preservation? "I promise I won't pass out, okay?"

Laced with frustrated anger, the words came out on a growl.

She reacted to his anger with her own. "Always with the promises. Just make sure you keep this one. I don't relish the thought of prying you off the floor and hauling you back to bed."

And then, thankfully, she left as the picture of her in her bed, of him in her bed, of them in her bed together, notched itself indelibly in his mind.

Too soon she was back, and Logan found himself wishing he'd never suggested the change of clothes.

Virginal white cotton had given him enough problems. At least the essential parts had been well covered. The red cotton knit tank top she'd slipped on and tucked into crinkly khaki boxer shorts added whole new vistas to the demands of his libido.

Much as he'd like to blame her, the problem lay entirely with him. She wasn't a tease. Nothing about the clothes were suggestive or provocative. Mothers sent their ten-year-old daughters to school in less. Grandmothers took in the sights at the Alamo in similar garb. It simply was that on Carmen—specifically on Carmen's curves—the effect was to fill him with aching desire.

Didn't she know what she did to a man? No, he decided, watching her set the table and work hard at avoiding his gaze. She didn't know. He suspected that was part of the reason he found this difficult.

She was so damn vulnerable, yet so desirable he knew his conscience wasn't strong enough to keep him from taking advantage.

Out of the blue, the conscience in question interjected a thought that broadsided him. Rico bled her dry of money. If he followed through, what he planned to take from her held far greater value.

He wanted more than sex. Hell, if sex was the only issue, this wouldn't be so difficult. What he truly wanted wasn't his to take. He wanted a taste of what she was offering Dallas. Love—unconditional, uncompromising, not a cover-up for ambition and greed; something that regardless of his wealth, he'd never had before.

And even sadder than his need was the knowledge that if he pressured her, she would let him take it all.

Suddenly he was angry with her for leaving herself so open to hurt. "Don't you ever get tired of taking care of other people's problems?"

She looked at him in leery silence before leaning close to set a salad plate at his place. "I don't. I don't do that," she said, and frowned as if that conclusion had never dawned on her.

"No? You take care of Rico. You're taking care of me. And when you aren't taking care of people at the hospital, you're volunteering your time at the free clinic."

"I love my work," she said—so defensively, he knew he had her thinking.

"Has it ever occurred to you that you might work too hard?"

Her gaze flashed to his, questioning, before she shrugged. "I'm doing fine." Not a trace of regret. Not a hint of self-pity.

"Don't you sometimes think you deserve better than you get? Doesn't it ever make you angry?"

She set a bowl of soup in front of him and moved quickly away. "I get exactly what I want. Personal satisfaction. Not everyone can make a difference in another person's life. I can. I do. Every day. I worked hard for my education, but I consider the opportunity a gift. I'm too grateful to take it for granted."

Coming from anyone else, those noble sentiments might have sounded insincere. Because they'd come from Carmen, Logan accepted them—though that didn't mean he excused her naïveté.

"Why aren't you married, Carmen?" he asked point-blank, surprising himself as much as her. "Why isn't someone taking care of you?"

"Well, I guess that's where I draw the line."

He tried not to be affected by her sadly poignant smile as she joined him at the table.

"To my way of thinking, it would probably turn out the other way around. I'd end up taking care of him."

He gave a soft huff of agreement. "I suspect you've got a point there," he said, glad to see she had some instincts for self-preservation after all, although he sincerely doubted they were strong enough.

"Not that I'd expect to be taken care of," she added, dragging his attention back to her mouth. "A relationship should be equal. Give and take."

What she hadn't said was more telling than what she had. He studied her lowered lashes, satin black, thick and lush, and he got lost for a moment in an image of those lashes lowered in anticipation of his kiss.

He forced himself to concentrate on the food she'd set in front of him. "Yet so far, where men are concerned, you've done all the giving and they've done all the taking, am I right?"

Her silence was his answer. Men were bastards. He ought to know. He was one of the worst. He clenched his jaw and looked away.

He scanned the sparsely furnished apartment. If she'd let him, he sure as hell could make her life easier.

Trying to buy your way out of the guilt? he asked himself darkly. At least he could do better by her than Dallas. While it was a given that he would leave her, he, at least, could compensate her. He told himself he would do just that, regardless of what happened or didn't happen between them.

Surely there were things she wanted. "Don't you ever wish for more, Carmen?" he asked.

She busied her hands breaking crackers into her soup, acting far too casual, far too unaffected by his insistent probing. "What is this, twenty questions?"

"Answer me," he pressed.

She sighed heavily. "More what?"

"More everything," he said expansively, his irritation with her total lack of greed getting tangled with his admiration for the very same quality. "Someone to take care of you for a change. Someone to give you things. Material things—you should have diamonds, Carmen. Instead you've been given coal."

Logan Prince didn't wax poetic. He told himself Johnny Dallas probably did and that he was only playing the role. The sweet, surprised smile tilting her mouth told him how good an actor he was.

Her look was both wistful and bittersweet for a moment before she manufactured a stage frown and touched her palm to his forehead. "You running a fever, Johnny? It's not like you to be so concerned about what I might need."

She was trying for cool, steady humor. The slight trembling of her hand told him she was neither cool nor steady. His preoccupation with this line of questioning told him he wasn't either.

"No fever," he said wearily, unable to dodge an unshakable guilt over his deception. "Maybe I just realized what a selfish, self-centered bastard I am. Maybe I'm thinking I've got a lot to be sorry for where you're concerned."

The sorrys hadn't even begun. Too much heat, too much fire came to flame when their gazes met. And every time she touched him, he damn near went up in smoke. He wasn't sure anymore if he could get out of this without hurting her. And he could see in her eyes that she was probably going to let him.

It made him angry. At himself and a past that had made him the cold, calculating opportunist he was today. And at her, for placing so little value on her self-worth and for wasting her love on a ne'er-do-well like Dallas. Oddly these thoughts fueled a need in him to give her what she deserved.

And what might that be, Prince? he asked himself. Does she deserve to be lied to and seduced by a man whose existence in her world is a lie?

"What about love, Carmen?" He watched her closely, damned if he knew why he was pushing these points. Damned if he knew why he was letting himself care. "Let's talk about that. You could have any man you wanted. Why do you think you want a man like me?"

She wouldn't look at him. And if he wasn't mistaken, it took all her will to keep from bolting out of the chair and running from the room.

"Why, Carmen?" he repeated, more gently but no less insistently.

She raised her chin and glared at him. "I'm glad to see those lumps you took didn't put any bruises in your ego."

He had to smile at her show of grit and blustery pride.

"Okay," he conceded, paying court to that pride. "For the sake of argument, let's say you have better judgment than to fall for a saddle tramp like me. What kind of a man would you fall in love with?"

Her quick, jerky motions told him she was wound as tight as a reel of microfiche.

He didn't want her to be so tense, though he also didn't want her calm. Despite all his noble words and convoluted thoughts on the subject, he wanted her aware of *him*. He wanted her wild and reckless, lost in love, lost in him. Lost in Logan Prince, not Johnny Dallas.

He closed his eyes and ran a hand through his hair in frustration. He was turned inside out by this woman. It wasn't like him. But then, he wasn't himself, was he? He was no longer Logan Prince, a ruthless, cold-blooded corporate raider. He was Johnny Dallas. A good-natured urban cowboy, quick with a grin, with time to kill and women to win.

He looked at the woman sitting across from him. The one who brought a flurry of emotions swirling like a dust devil on a dry Texas plain. The one who made him as attuned to his needs as a man as he was attuned to hers as a woman . . . and he couldn't stop wondering what it would take for Logan Prince to win her.

Bullying wouldn't do the trick. He decided to back off—at least until he was capable of thinking straight.

"Look. Forget it. Forget I asked," he said, then winced when he drew in too deep a breath. "Forget this whole conversation. It's none of my business anyway what you do, or what you want."

She looked as confused as he felt. He didn't like the fact that she prompted this acute sexual need, this sensation of new life from feelings he'd thought were dead inside him, this unsettling focus on longings he'd stowed away behind the man-of-steel image.

The man of steel fought a slow but undeniable melting as she watched him with wary concern.

Damn, he was tired. And confused. He fought both weaknesses and took refuge in the notion that the residual effects of the beating he'd taken were responsible for his state of mind.

"You're right about one thing," he said wearily. "I think it's time I got back to bed."

When she folded her napkin beside her plate and came to his side, he didn't fight her. With her help he stood, then let her lead him back to her bed, where he collapsed and fell into a restless sleep.

Night shadows whispered like mist through the bedroom and danced with the dreamy glow of the neon light blinking softly but steadily through the curtains covering the window. Logan fought to hang on to the oblivion of sleep, where he could hide a little longer from the pain.

Sweat soaked his body. Sleep drifted farther away and with it the numb relief it offered; a fragrance drifted nearer. Her fragrance.

He opened his eyes and looked toward the door to see her standing there.

Carmen. His silken angel. His steady strength. His uncommon weakness.

She'd undone her hair. And it could be his undoing.

The first time he'd seen her thick black braid falling across her shoulder, he'd wanted to see that glorious hair unbound. He'd wanted to see it brushing across the honey-colored slope of her breasts so he could brush them with his fingers, then his mouth. . . .

He swallowed thickly at the sight of her hair cascading about her face, tumbling wildly over her shoulders and down her back, sleep-mussed, shining— in need of a man's hands to add to the paganly elegant disarray.

In need of his hands.

He knotted his fists into the sheets at either side of his hips as she hesitated in the doorway, her shadow falling softly across the foot of the bed.

She was so still as she stood there, watching him, waiting. Her sleep shirt had slipped off the delicate slope of one shoulder. Backlit as she was by dim light and shadows, the thin cotton provided little more than a film that caressed her body.

Her breasts sweetly filled the stretchy fabric. The velvet tips of her nipples crowned dark, dusky aureoles that strained against the cream-colored cotton. Silken shadows defined the sweet concave between fragile ribs and tiny waist, and lower, where the faint line of French-cut bikini panties left little else to the imagination. The shirt ended where hip met thigh, gently molding the slender curve of her bottom, revealing completely the long length of her legs.

Her skin was satin smooth and flawless, the color of butter caramels. He grew ravenous looking at her.

He tried to speak her name through tight, dry lips and a parched throat.

She moved quickly to his side. "You . . . you cried out in your sleep," she whispered, searching his face. "The pain . . . is it bad?"

He managed to shake his head. A huge silent lie.

She didn't buy it. "I'll be right back."

Silk and sex and sultry nights. That's what her voice made him think of. The low, heavy ache in his loins established its dominance among all the others as he waited in the darkness.

Aware of the deepness of the night.

Aware of how completely they were alone and of a need greater than any he'd ever known.

In his mind's eye, he saw again the way the light had intimately caressed the shadowed curves of her body. In his mind's eye, he saw his hands replacing the light.

She slipped to his side. Quiet. Efficient. All business. All bluff. All woman. Temptation incarnate.

She eased a hip next to his on the bed. Her slight weight pulled the sheet snugly across his hips, tightening the pressure against an arousal he couldn't have tempered if he'd tried.

"Take this. It's a painkiller," she whispered, and

carefully tucked the pill between his lips. He gripped her wrist, steadying her hand as she brought a glass to his mouth. Watching her face, he chased down the tablet with water.

She set the glass on the nightstand and touched a hand to his face. Cool hand. Soft. Trembling.

He reached without thought and covered it with his own.

Her hushed words made him a promise. "You'll start to feel better tomorrow, Johnny."

Johnny. Jealousy seared through Logan like a flash fire. It was not an emotion with which he felt remotely comfortable. Not an emotion he wished to feel. He'd never had the need. What he'd wanted he'd bought, bartered for, or taken. In the case of women, whatever he'd wanted had been freely given. But never had it been given from the heart.

Dallas had this woman's heart. In spite of Logan's intentions not to hurt her, envy goaded him into finding out what prize came with that possession.

"Tomorrow," she repeated with soft, sweet assurance as he wrapped his fingers possessively around her small wrist and pulled her toward him.

"Tonight," he whispered, meeting her shadowed gaze and seeing that she understood what his harsh whisper suggested. "Tonight."

Her eyes glistened with a hundred questions, a thousand longings, a very real conviction that she knew giving in to him would be a mistake. The floral scent of her hair brushed across his face, as black as midnight, as delicate as moonglow. She slowly shook her head, denying his gruff command.

He'd never pleaded with a woman. So he wasn't sure, exactly, what pushed him over the edge. His own need perhaps, which was so much stronger than any he'd ever felt. A wanting as profound and as demanding as any he'd ever known.

He touched a hand to her hair, threaded its satin weight through his fingers, then knotted a handful in his fist.

"Lie down with me." Grave with urgency, raspy with wanting, his voice betrayed his deep and wild need.

In the dark, in a silence interrupted only by the sweet, unsteady cadence of her breathing, he waited. Watching her eyes, tugging her closer, he counted on her feelings for Johnny Dallas to persuade her.

"Lie down with me. I want you near. Just for a little while."

He'd known she wouldn't deny him. He'd known and he'd used that knowledge like a lever.

She searched his face, hesitated, then eased down on the bed beside him.

It was painfully obvious to Logan that her action was prompted by love. He could feel it in the careful way she settled her head beside his on the pillow. He could see it in her dark gaze that pleaded and cared and agonized over her decision to give in to him while she knew it would be wiser to walk away.

Suddenly it didn't matter that he was a charlatan, a fraud. Suddenly he didn't care that it was Dallas's wish she was granting. It only mattered that she was with him.

When she surrendered, he embraced the warmth her lush curves offered. Sinking into her healing heat, he buried his mouth in her hair.

It was devastatingly humbling, this feeling he had holding her. Here in his arms was a woman whose sole motivation for lying with him was to give. Against her better judgment, she'd come to him. Against all odds, he was deeply touched by the gesture.

So this is what it felt like when a woman gave without guile, he thought. This was what it felt like when a woman offered without expectation. A gift without a trade-off. Such a basic instinct for a woman like Carmen.

A natural gesture for her.

A rare experience for him.

He closed his eyes and felt an odd thickness in his throat. He swallowed it back, clenching his jaw against the flood of emotions this woman caused to swell inside him.

Nothing but her thin sleep shirt was between them. Her shirt and her uncertainty. And, suddenly—unexpectedly—his conscience also wedged its way between them too.

Amazing. When had it gotten so strong? Somewhere between sitting in her kitchen and watching her prepare his supper? Somewhere between telling her she deserved better than what she got and plotting to give her even worse?

Somewhere between her giving and his dawning determination not to take.

She was everything soft and sensual pressed against him. Everything warm and real. And though he was anything but immune to the subtle shifting of her unbound breasts, the satin length of her legs aligned with his, his heart reacted to her needs.

Did he want her physically? Only as badly as he wanted to breathe. And no matter how many times he'd told himself he would take her, he realized that he couldn't.

He was going to take care of her instead. It was past time someone did.

She was exhausted. Physically. Emotionally. He'd known, and he'd deliberately taken advantage, sensing she'd lie down with him simply because he'd asked her to. Because she thought she was doing something for him—*for Johnny*, he corrected himself. Grating as that conclusion was, he wasn't going to let it sway him.

He'd known it would never occur to her that she needed this from him as well. It would never occur to her that for once, someone other than she was going to do the giving. But it occurred to him. It was the first time in recent memory that he'd manipulated someone into doing something strictly for selfless reasons.

Along with all the other feelings, she prompted that long-lost need in him too. He was still in a quandary as to why. Her innocence for one thing. And maybe he admired her naïveté more than he was willing to admit. A quality that rare deserved something more than to be taken advantage of.

He eased his arm around her shoulders and drew her against him.

"Johnny . . ." she whispered, her body tensing, her eyes growing wary.

"Shhh." He brushed the hair back from her face, then slowly stroked her arm from shoulder to wrist. Lacing his fingers with hers, he drew their joined hands to his chest. "Shhh. Just sleep. Just lie here and sleep with me."

He felt her slowly relax beside him. And fought the temptation to lose himself completely in her softness. Telling himself he couldn't afford to get lost anyway. Denying the fact that he already had.

He couldn't afford to get lost in anything. Especially not in a woman. Most specifically not a woman like Carmen.

She needed passion and promises. Whatever passion he'd once had was long buried under layers of corporate responsibility and calculated control. Whatever promises he could make hinged on the swing of the Dow Jones average.

She needed commitment and caring. He was committed to Prince Enterprises. As for caring, he simply didn't have in him. Thirty days from now he was going to walk away. He'd go back to his world and leave her to hers.

That reality troubled him far more than it should have.

She fell asleep long before he did. Long before he quit questioning his motives, which were as uncharacteristic as they were confusing. Long before he accepted that Johnny Dallas, a drifter and a wastrel, owned this woman's heart.

Too long he lay in the dark, brooding, resentful, convinced that despite his own fortune and power, that precious possession made Dallas the wealthier man.

He slept, although he wasn't sure when, for all the thinking he'd done. By dawn, after a night with Carmen nestled in his arms, he'd realized that as consciences went, his was long on good intentions and short on staying power.

Midnight conviction was no match for the needs she'd resurrected, needs that had come to full realization in this pearly blush of morning. Midnight conviction was no deterrent to a desire only she could satisfy.

Everything about Carmen Sanchez was real. He'd never had that from a woman before.

He had it now. He wanted to hold on to it. And somewhere between darkness and dawn, that want had grown into an obsession.

He wanted to taste it. To hold it in his hands. He wanted to feel it. Breathe it. Savor every nuance, every sigh, every giving, selfless feeling for what it was.

Fully awake, fully aroused, he ran his hand from the elegant length of her back to the slender curve of her hip.

She sighed and snuggled closer. The leg that she'd slung across his hips in her sleep pressed against his erection.

He clenched his jaw at the sweet torture and cupped her face in his hand. Her skin was velvet soft, her breath whisper light and sweetly fragile against his jaw. Threading his fingers through her hair, he tested its weight, drowning in its texture before gathering a handful in his fist and tilting her face gently toward his.

Reluctantly, lazily, she came awake. Slowly, then wonderingly, she became aware of the intent in his gaze, the heat of his body, of the strength of his arousal beneath her leg.

Such fire flared in her eyes. Such sweet anticipation and glittering awareness. Such trust.

He closed his eyes, not wanting to see that trust as he drew her against him.

"Just a kiss," he whispered against her mouth, telling himself that was as far as it would go.

She hovered hesitantly above him, the delicacy of her breath feathering across his lips a gentle torture, a powerful seduction.

With tender care, she lowered her head and pressed her lips to his. Exquisitely gentle, undeniably shy, it was more of a dance than a kiss. Her mouth moved over his with graceful rhythms, shivery sighs, subtle shiftings. And her question became a plea underscored with simmering heat and morning desire.

His low groan of response gave her confidence. He could see it in her eyes as she levered herself above him. The flat of her hands pressed into the mattress on either side of his chest. The soft crush of her breasts against his chest inflamed him.

"Your mouth . . ." she whispered, then placed the lightest of kisses to the swollen flesh. "I don't want to hurt you."

"Hurt me," he said fiercely, then surprised them both with a shadow of a grin. "When you hurt me like that, it feels too good."

Her tentative smile told him she was having difficulty believing she could provoke that response. She lowered her mouth again and, emboldened by his restless yearning, experimented with the satin glide of her tongue against his teeth.

"Better than good," he whispered harshly. Cradling her head in his hands, he drew her into a deep, drugging kiss.

There were so many textures to this woman. So many tastes. All of them heaven. All of them hell on a man who wanted to take charge but had to pander to his injuries and let her set the pace.

If he hadn't been flat on his back, she'd have brought him to his knees as she scattered long, lingering kisses across his brow. He sucked in his breath when she brushed her lips in a slow, teasing slide down his cheek, nuzzling, tasting, scraping the underside of his jaw with her tongue. He groaned at the whispers of sensation from her mouth and the gentle friction of her breasts moving across his chest as she stretched to gain better access.

Untangling his hands from her hair, he framed her slim shoulders lightly before grasping her ribs. In silent awe, he explored her fragile bone structure, her slender hips. He pressed the heels of his hands against the plump sides of her breasts. She was small everywhere but there. The contrast was stunningly erotic and made a shambles of his resolve not to take this any farther.

She made a soft, urgent whimper when he wedged his hands between their chests and strafed her nipples with his thumbs. Beneath the thin cotton, her nipples hardened. Beneath the sheet that had slipped low on his hips, his arousal responded in kind.

He groaned and spanned her ribs with his hands, spreading his fingers wide. Quickly she pulled away, her dark eyes clouded with questions and uncertainty.

"Did I hurt you?" she asked, her hands skillfully checking his bandaged ribs.

He shook his head and reached for the hem of her shirt. "I want to see you."

Her hands stilled, as did his heart when their gazes locked.

This was all wrong. But it was moving too fast for

him to stall it. He saw the desire laced with hesitation on her face, and he couldn't stop himself from wanting another taste of her.

"Shhh . . ." He drew her gently toward him. "It's all right." He smoothed the sleep shirt back over her hips, then watched with a tightening in his chest as she brushed her hair away from her face. One long heavy strand escaped to cascade over her breast and curled provocatively over the cotton-covered tip of a dusky-brown nipple.

She was stunningly beautiful. Achingly unsure. He told her with his eyes, showed her with his touch how incredibly lovely, how impossibly exotic he found her.

He reached for her and praised her with his gaze when she didn't pull away. His hands were large. Her breasts filled his palms with pliant heat, pillow softness. Every pulse point in his body thrummed with desire as he watched his fingers caress, and mold, and play across her flesh until her nipples pearled to ridged peaks beneath her shirt.

Her eyes grew slumberous and dark, so dark, as with a gentle pressure of his hands he drew her toward his mouth. "I want to taste you," he whispered, and her expression told him she wanted it too.

Honeyed velvet sheathed in a wisp of cotton skimmed across his lips as he closed his mouth around her. He arched his neck, reaching, seeking as he lowered his hands to her waist and urged her closer.

Even through the shirt, her texture and weight was incomparably sweet, a delicious taste of forbidden fruit, a sultry promise, an elusive temptation.

Beneath his hands, he felt her delicate shivers, her shimmering sighs. She leaned closer, then rose to her knees and, planting her hands on the pillow on either side of his head, straddled him. Her knees sank into the mattress as she closeted his hips between her thighs.

Logan had hungered before, but never like he hungered for this woman. Braced on hands and knees above him, her hair tumbling wildly about her face, her back arched, she looked both pagan and pure.

The tips of her breasts strained against the cotton that was wet from the caress of his mouth. The fabric molded to her nipple, as revealing as bare skin and, if possible, more erotic as she brushed her nipple across his lips . . . teasing him . . . tempting him.

He recaptured a distended nipple between his lips, laving it with his tongue, sipping, suckling, drawing her into his mouth with uncommon gentleness—then insatiable greed.

He opened his eyes, wanting to see her face as he loved her. A soft "oh" of desire formed on her sweetly parted lips as her eyes drifted shut and her thick lashes swept down onto her flushed cheeks.

He tunneled his hands under her shirt and filled them with the generous weight of her breasts. Breathless and needy, she offered yet more of herself, throwing her head back, arching the satin length of her neck, straining for more of what he was doing to her.

Her responses were wildly provocative. Brazenly lusty. Yet so honest and natural, he lost himself in her taste and her giving. He felt himself slip faster, deeper into a desire that blended sweetly with surrender—his own surrender.

He didn't ask this time. He tugged the shirt above her breasts and took her into his mouth. When he bit her lightly, she gasped and offered yet more. He took it all and, in the taking, took care to give her pleasure.

"Johnny . . ."

It was barely a whisper . . . an impassioned plea . . . another man's name.

Logan froze. Something heavy and cold settled deep inside him. Something hollow and cutting. Something painfully real to remind him she was responding to another man.

He tried to tell himself it didn't matter. But it did. It mattered a lot.

And it was something he simply couldn't bear.

FOUR

Carmen struggled to catch her breath. Heat shivered through her body in delicious, mind-stealing waves as Johnny sucked and tugged and made sweet love to her breast. She felt limp and liquid, totally immersed in sensation and in the feel of his large, strong hands clamped possessively at her waist.

She hadn't known it could be like this. She'd never dreamed she could feel so much. Or that a man could want her the way this man was wanting her now. Nor had she imagined the power he'd have over her when it finally happened.

She felt suspended somewhere between heaven and earth, flying free with uninhibited desire, ready to give herself body and soul.

It was intoxicating, this longing, this insatiable craving for more of anything and everything he wanted to do with her. She wanted it to go on forever. She wanted to believe it would, wanted it so badly that when he stopped, she fought the notion that something had very abruptly, very definitely changed between them.

Dazed with desire, she slowly opened her eyes. What she saw in his confirmed what she'd been trying to deny. He wasn't with her anymore. He was as still as silence beneath her. His face was as hard as stone. The blue flame in his eyes had cooled to glacial hardness.

Like awakening from a warm, seductive dream to a cold, empty bed, she felt suddenly vulnerable, excruciatingly exposed. She searched his face for answers. Nothing but expressionless, icy silence met her gaze.

"What it is? Are you hurting? Oh, dear God, did I hurt you?"

"No. You didn't hurt me." He drew a deep breath and set her away from him. "Carmen . . . look, I don't think this is such a good idea," he said flatly.

In slow, deliberate motion, he covered his eyes with his forearm rather than look at her. Disguised as a gentle dismissal, it was nonetheless an arrow that found its mark and pierced her heart.

On this July morning that promised a day as hot as any Texas summer day could be, the room chilled by several degrees. Slowly, in a wounded daze, she eased away from him. Stunned and suddenly embarrassed, she tugged her sleep shirt down over her hips. The tremors that had begun to shake her body made the simple task difficult.

"I—I'm sorry," she murmured, at a loss to know what to do, what to say.

"Yeah, well, I guess that makes two of us."

If he'd struck her, he couldn't have hurt her more. He was sorry. And she was a fool.

She shut her eyes as her mind cleared of passion and painted a vivid picture of what had just happened between them.

What had she been thinking? This was exactly what she'd been determined to avoid. She'd let her compassion for his pain get in the way of her common sense. She'd let her needs and her desire for him override her resolve to avoid a one-night stand, a one-night stand that in this harsh light of morning, he'd decided wasn't worth the effort.

Her stomach clenched when she thought of the way she'd practically attacked him, willing to give herself to him completely.

But he'd seemed so different when he'd reached for her. The bold, brassy, don't-give-a-damn Johnny hadn't been making love to her. A needy, sadly vulnerable, soul-touchingly lost man had turned to her in the most elemental of ways. She'd reacted instinctively. She'd read something in the way he'd looked at her, something in the way he'd touched her that had led her to believe he was finally seeing her for what she was: A woman he could love. And that he could be the man she could count on to treasure the love she could give him.

She'd been wrong. What happened between them had been physical. Nothing more. Nothing meaningful. And when he'd stopped to consider who he was with, weighed the outcome, he'd opted to beg off.

How he must pity the poor little sex-starved goody-two-shoes. Sick with self-loathing, she swung her feet to the floor, driven by a violent urge to run away.

He reached out and snagged her wrist. "Carmen . . ."

In agonized silence she waited, not daring to look at him. She didn't want to see the pity in his eyes.

"You think you want this," he said finally, in a controlled, emotionless voice, "but I promise you that you really don't. I'm not what you need. And I'm a hell of a lot less than you deserve. I never should have let this happen."

Somehow his attempt to shoulder the blame cut deeper than his rejection. She closed her eyes, squeezing back the threat of tears. She wasn't going to add to her humiliation by letting him see her cry.

"It's all right, Johnny. You don't have to make excuses. And you don't have to explain. You were hurting. I was here. It's that simple."

She saw it all with brutal clarity now. She was a warm body. A healing heat. Nothing special. Merely available—like so many others.

"Any old port in a storm, and all that," she added, working too hard to dodge the pain that came with the realization. "Don't worry about it, okay? It's no big thing."

She rose, and this time when he would have stopped her, she forcefully pried his hand off her wrist.

"I've got to go." She walked on unsteady legs to the door. "Get some sleep. I'll be back in a couple of hours."

Logan made a decision somewhere after dawn, a time that had almost been destructive. Whether pride played a bigger part in his decision than nobility, he wasn't sure. Certainly it had hurt to hear himself called by another man's name. He only knew for sure that if it took every ounce of resolve, he was not going to use Carmen. She'd been used enough. And he'd done more than his share of using already. Dallas sure as hell didn't deserve her, but neither did she deserve losing the intimacy and trust Logan had almost taken from her this morning. Bottom line, those emotions weren't his to take.

Yet when he thought of the way she'd responded to him, he ached in places that had nothing to do with the beating he'd taken. When he recalled the look on her face when he'd all but thrown her out of her own bed, he hurt in places that had nothing to do with physical pain.

He could have told her the truth then. He should have told her. But he'd lain there, listening to her shower, then faking sleep when she'd come back into the bedroom to gather clean clothes. And then he'd let her leave without offering a word of explanation.

He'd thought he could take without giving.

She'd proven him wrong.

He'd thought he could experience without involvement.

She'd blasted that foolish notion to hell and back.

He'd tasted her passion. He'd felt the burn of her desire. And if there'd been one truth implied or spoken between them this morning in her bed, it was that she should have far better than he was capable of giving her.

So he was going to leave her alone, knowing that if he tried to lose her memory in a thousand women in the future, he would be haunted forever by her wild, uninhibited responses, her reckless yearning, and her sweet innocence. And forever he'd wish she'd been making love with Logan Prince this morning, not Johnny Dallas.

Precious and rare was the sense of total union they'd shared. He'd been completely lost in her, submerged and sinking deeper into a realm of sensation that for the first time in his life had more substance than cynicism, more sharing than greed.

The real thing. He'd held it in his hands. He'd felt it in his heart.

He'd watched it walk away.

As he lay there, wondering at his motives and questioning his sanity, he realized he had to get out of her life. This entire charade was beginning to reek of lunacy anyway. His thoughts might be a little muddled where Carmen was concerned, but he was beginning to think a little more clearly in other areas.

He must have been insane even to propose trading

places with Dallas. His only defense was his physical condition. Pain played games with the mind. He'd been looking for an escape and the bluff had provided the most direct route. It had also turned out to be a disastrous one.

Long after he was sure Carmen had left the apartment, he rose from her bed. Long after he realized she'd been right that he was starting to feel better, he placed a call to Ben.

By the time he hung up, his suspicions were confirmed. Things weren't working well on that end either.

Ben had been frantic and so damn glad to hear from him, Logan had thought the man was going to cry. As Ben had so bluntly phrased it, "This Prince-and-the-Pauper routine may have played well for Mark Twain, but it's not cutting it for Prince Enterprises."

It wasn't that Dallas wasn't giving it his best shot. It wasn't even that Ben couldn't handle the specifics of the Kramer-Carmichael merger, or a hundred other major and minor decisions bound to come up in the course of a month. Instead it was something that neither of them had been able to anticipate, but should have guessed.

Preston Prince was coming home three weeks early, and he was demanding an audience with his son.

Assuring Ben he needed just a few days more to give his face time to heal and then he'd step back into character, Logan hung up; he knew what he had to do.

He stood in Carmen's shower, letting the spray and steam ease some of the aches from his body while another ache built in his chest.

He had four days. In four days he'd lose his freedom. Significant as that may have seemed when this charade began, the real significance was outweighed by another factor.

In four days he was going to lose Carmen.

Letting go of something he'd never really had shouldn't seem like such a loss. Yet it did. In spades.

He reached for the faucets and twisted them off. For a long moment he stood there staring at the shower stall as water dripped in his eyes and the bitter taste of self-pity welled up in his throat. He quickly swallowed it back, along with his cynical pride.

Oh well. At best it had been a long shot. He told himself he'd have probably tired of the game long before the month was over anyway.

With a deep, weary sigh, he shoved back the shower curtain and reached for a towel. Knotting it at his hips and avoiding looking at himself in the steamy mirror, he stepped out into the hall—and directly into a waist-high version of a clinging vine.

Catching his balance with a hand against the door-jamb, Logan looked down on the shining black hair covering the head of a little boy who had clamped short, sadly slender arms around his thighs like a pair of vise grips.

"What the—"

"Oh dear."

He snapped his head up at the sound of Carmen's voice.

Their gazes met and held for a speaking moment. Her dark eyes revealed how hurt she felt. In silence, he tried, with a look, to tell her he was sorry. But looks weren't going to help any more than words would set it right.

Pride made her lift her chin. She graced him with a small smile. I'm a survivor, it said and it'll take a lot more than a busted-up cowboy with testosterone flooding his brain to get me down.

He prayed to a God he hadn't given much thought to of late that she was as tough as she'd like him to think she was.

"Juan," she said, turning her attention and her energy to the business of prying the little boy away from Logan's legs. "Honey, let Johnny go."

Juan wasn't about to budge. The child clung like a seasoned rider on the back of a bronc. When it became apparent he wasn't going to let go, Carmen tried to reason with him.

Dropping to her knees, she spoke slowly and patiently to the boy. "Juan, you've got to be careful. Remember what I told you? Johnny was in an accident. He's not feeling so good. Honey, you've got to let go."

If possible, the little arms tightened their grip around his thighs.

"Juan, Johnny can't walk if you don't let him go."

As exasperating as the situation was, Logan felt an

oddly disturbing pang of compassion for the child. He didn't have a clue as to what to do. He'd never been around children. For that matter, he hadn't ever really given them much thought. The thought that struck him now, though, was that he felt like an anchor and this child was adrift at sea.

"I'm sorry," Carmen whispered, looking up at him. "He was so worried about you when I told him you'd been hurt."

Her gaze drifted quickly over Logan's bare chest, where beads of water from his shower still pearled in springy curls. His heart pounded heavily at her sweeping, visual caress.

"I'm glad to see you're up. Are you . . . are you feeling better?" She stared at the towel knotted at his hips before quickly looking again at his face.

"Yes. Much better. The shower made me feel almost human."

He couldn't help but notice the deep flush on her cheeks as her gaze darted again to his chest, to the slipping towel, then back to the boy.

"Good. That's good. If you could just let him know you're okay, I think we could get him to let go—at least until you put some clothes on."

Logan gripped the towel, knotting the corners in his fist before it slipped past the point of total exposure. It wouldn't do for either of them to witness the physical evidence of what the look in her dark eyes was doing to him.

He glanced down at the child and, after a moment's

hesitation, surprised himself by touching his other hand to the boy's hair. Juan craned his neck, looked up at Logan with huge black eyes filled with far too much trust. They looked achingly troubled and claimed ownership of wisdom far beyond their years.

Shaking off that puzzling thought, he forced a smile. "It's all right, Juan." His voice sounded curiously gruff, even to his own ears. "You don't have to worry about me. I'm okay. Even if I look a little dented around the edges."

The child continued to stare up at him and, after a long moment of indecision, lowered his head and clung even tighter.

Confused, completely out of his element, Logan let his frustration show. "What the devil's going on here?"

Carmen's gaze swung to his, a perplexing frown on her face. He could see from her expression that he'd made a major blunder. Whatever connection Dallas had to this child, it was binding. His continued ineptness at handling the boy's distress would give him away before he had the chance to tell her the truth about who he was. And the truth was the least of the debts he felt he owed her.

Carefully prying the small arms from around his legs, he faced the child squarely. "Come on, Juan. I'm okay. You think old Johnny would let anything bad happen to him? That wouldn't work, now, would it? If I let anything happen to me, I wouldn't get to see you, now, would I? And that would never do."

The scrawny arms relaxed. The pinched frown on Juan's face, however, stayed in place.

What the hell did kids react to, anyway? Logan wondered in frustration. Then he thought of Ruby. More than a housekeeper, more often than not his only family when he was growing up with a mother and a father who were rarely present, Ruby used to make him cookies when he was a kid. Ruby and her cookies had pulled him out of many a blue funk. Surely that time-honored tradition still held some clout.

"Come on, partner. I'll bet Carmen can find you some cookies while I get my pants on. Right, Carmen?" he asked, praying he'd said the right thing.

Evidently he had, because while she still looked at him a bit oddly, she was smiling.

She touched Juan's shoulder, getting his attention. "Johnny's right, Juan. I've got your favorite. How about some chocolate-chip cookies and a glass of milk?"

It looked as if the cookies were going to do the trick. After giving Logan one last, measuring look, Juan let go, put his small hand in Carmen's, and let her lead him toward the kitchen.

Logan stared after them, wondering what had just happened, remembering Dallas's explanation of Carmen's generosity: . . . *if a lost child needed mending* . . .

Juan must be one of those lost children he'd been referring to.

After he'd dressed in another pair of Dallas's faded jeans and a dark cotton T-shirt, Logan made his way slowly into the kitchen to join them. Juan was well into his glass of milk. By the telltale crumbs on the plate in front him, he'd evidently polished off a fair share of cookies to boot.

Carmen sat at the table beside him, watching him, her hands wrapped loosely around a coffee mug.

Logan eased into a chair, quietly assessing the situation. As if he'd been waiting for that move, Juan scooted down from his chair and slipped to Logan's side without uttering a sound. After staring silently up at Logan for several long, searching moments, Juan leaned against him, his small hands resting on Logan's thigh.

Totally at a loss, Logan looked to Carmen for guidance.

She wasn't about to give it. As quiet as Juan, she watched and waited.

It seemed there was nothing left for him to do. Feeling clumsy, but driven by compassion, he eased his arm around the boy's small shoulders and gave him a brief, solid hug.

The silent communication must have been the reassurance the child needed. He looked up into Logan's eyes and smiled. A big, trusting, contented smile that put a lump in Logan's throat and spread an unfamiliar warmth through his chest. Instinct took over then. He ruffled the boy's hair then turned to Carmen.

"You've got a man here who could go for some milk and cookies too. How 'bout it?" he added when she just sat there, tears gathering in her eyes, a sweet smile of praise spreading over her face.

If he had known, if he'd had a clue what that smile was capable of doing to his insides, he'd have found a way to prompt it much, much sooner. He'd have gone to great lengths, in fact, to see it long before this.

In the next moment he realized he'd have been better off if he'd never seen her smile at him that way—as if he'd made her happy beyond measure, as if he'd said something wonderful and selfless and wise. It was one more memory he'd have to deal with when he left her.

Juan picked that moment to turn to Carmen. Logan watched, a confused frown deepening to a scowl as the little boy began to make slow, painfully meticulous formations with his fingers. The gestures, though strange to watch and seemingly meaningless at first, gradually took on significance. They weren't meaningless at all. In fact, it became glaringly clear how much meaning they had. The boy was signing.

His heart sank as it all made sense. The silence, the intense stares, the way Carmen looked directly at him when she spoke to him. Juan wasn't silent out of shyness. He was silent because he was deaf.

Logan raised stricken eyes to Carmen. She was smiling. So broadly. So proudly. She gave Juan a quick, loving hug then set him away from her and answered him in sign language.

Stalled somewhere between compassion and a

crippling sense of dread, Logan managed to form a question.

"What did he say?"

She gave Juan another quick, prideful smile then turned that smile on Logan. "He said, 'You make great cookies, Mom.' "

Mom? The word reverberated through Logan's head like a freight train thundering over rough rails. *Mom.* He closed his eyes, cursing Johnny Dallas for this *slight* omission about Carmen's background. Then he cursed himself for his brilliant deception.

Carmen had a child. A deaf child.

What the hell had he gotten himself into?

Several stunned moments passed before he realized she'd given up and a tear had escaped to spill freely down her cheek.

"It doesn't make any sense, I know," she said, swiping it away, then turning her back so neither Juan nor Logan could see her face. "Crying I mean."

When she got herself under control, she turned back to him, a tremulous smile hovering on her lips. "It's only that it's the first time he's ever signed for me. I've waited so long to have him talk to me. It . . ." She paused, warding off a renewed threat of tears. "It's been so hard not having him here. Wondering— always wondering if he's okay when he's away."

Her gaze swung to his, a little wide with elation, a little glazed with lingering doubts.

"I miss him so much. Every time I bring him here

for a visit, it gets harder to take him back to the group home."

Still stunned, still absorbing, Logan listened in silence while she talked. He was still having difficulty with the fact that she had a child. Not only a child, but a deaf child.

"It's been hard on him too. But seeing him sign . . ." She paused and tousled Juan's dark head as she set another plate of cookies on the table. "Maybe it's all been worth it. They're helping him."

Logan inched out of shock enough to see from the look in her eyes that she still questioned if she was doing the right thing. He didn't think about perimeters or consequences or the wisdom of keeping his distance. He simply acted on an uncompromising urge to reassure her.

He held out his hand. "Come here."

She moved hesitantly to his side.

Drawing her to him, he buried his face in the softness of her belly and wrapped his arms around her hips. "You are doing exactly the right thing. He needs this from you. And as much as you want him with you, you need this for him too."

He had no idea where the words had come from. His heart, probably, he decided, resigned but no longer surprised.

Her hands fell lightly to his shoulders before she drew his head against her with a gentle caress of her hands in his hair.

"Thank you," she whispered. "I needed to hear that."

He couldn't stop himself. He nuzzled his face into the pillow of her breasts, absorbing her warmth, wallowing in her softness, remembering her taste.

Warmth spread through him as he held her. It had little to do with chemistry; it had everything to do with caring. Warning signals started to sound at the same time he felt her stiffen, as if she'd just realized what they were inviting. As if she'd just remembered the intimacies they'd shared and the blow he'd landed to her fragile ego.

She made to pull away.

He stopped her and held her fast. "Carmen, about this morning. Please believe me when I tell you that I didn't want what was happening between us to stop."

He felt the muscles of her abdomen tense against his jaw, felt her hands drop from his hair to rest limply on his shoulders.

"I told you, you don't have to explain," she insisted.

It was time he told her the truth. "Yes, I do. I wanted you. I still want you. But I'm not the man you think I am. I'm not the man you want me to be." He let her go then, needing to see her face, needing to see her anger when he made his confession.

But she looked so vulnerable and so open to hurt, he realized right then that he couldn't tell her. Not now, at any rate.

"I'm not the man you need," he said finally. It was a compromise, but that much at least was true. "I never will be."

She wanted to say something. He saw it in her eyes. But he also saw how much hurt it caused her and let it drop. When her eyes registered recognition of his intent, he was glad he did.

This wasn't the time. This was the time she need to enjoy her son. *Her son.* That revelation was still giving him some problems.

He looked from her to Juan. "How long has it been since you've seen him?"

"Two weeks," she said quickly, making it sound like it had been two years. "They—the people at the group home—say it's best that way. I'm beginning to believe them." Her gaze caressed the boy.

"But, like you said," he added, finishing her thought for her, "it's hard."

She nodded. Her gaze darted to his then back to Juan.

"He looks good, doesn't he?"

Logan studied the child. Juan looked, he decided, revisiting his earlier assessment, like a child who was wise beyond his years. He really couldn't see a resemblance to Carmen. Maybe he favored his father.

A tightening in his gut told him that was a line of thought he'd be better off steering clear of. He didn't like to think of her with another man who touched her the way he had touched her this morning, making a baby with her.

In brooding silence, he studied Juan. While he'd initially thought he was painfully thin, he could see now that he was built on the wiry side. His skin glowed with vitality and health, his black hair was shiny bright.

"How long do you get to keep him?"

"Until tomorrow."

"You don't have to work?"

She shook her head. "Not until tomorrow night. I traded shifts with Barb. She owed me one."

He suspected that a lot of people owed Carmen.

He owed her too. Before he left her, he'd somehow figure out a way to pay his debt in full. That didn't mean it was going to make it any easier to walk away.

She touched Juan's shoulder. When she had his attention, she spoke slowly. At the same time she expertly signed the words. "Are you ready to go to the museum?"

Juan nodded enthusiastically, then cast an expectant grin toward Logan.

Logan didn't have to know sign language to understand what the child was asking. More dangerous melting took place in his chest.

Damn, he had to get out of here before he discovered more soft spots in his armor, more weaknesses.

"Tell him I'd like to go," he said gruffly, "but that I'm not quite ready for a day on the town."

"You tell him," she said, slanting him a puzzled frown. "If you speak slowly, he can read your lips."

Disappointment clouded Juan's eyes when Logan slowly and distinctly told him he couldn't go.

"Maybe if Johnny rests this afternoon, he can

play Chutes and Ladders with you for a little while tonight."

She glanced at Logan, her brows raised hopeful-ly.

"Sure," he heard himself saying when a smile brightened Juan's face. "As long as you promise not to beat me too badly, okay?" He'd worry later about the fact that he didn't have a clue as to what he'd just agreed to do.

Juan's grin widened as he signed the word *okay*.

With concentrated effort, and not stopping to analyze what possessed him, Logan made a clumsy attempt to sign the word right back.

He must have gotten his message across because both Carmen and Juan were beaming at him when he finished.

Feeling inordinately pleased with himself, then self-conscious, he mumbled something about needing to lie down and left them.

When he heard the door shut behind them, he lay down on the bed, stacked his hands behind his head, and stared at the ceiling.

Maybe it was a good thing this charade was going to be cut short, he told himself darkly. He needed to get back to the things that were important to him. Back to the things that mattered. Money. Power. Control. Those tangible constants that moved the world and kept him from thinking about alternatives. Alternatives like involvement with a trusting little boy whose smile did the most incredible things to his heart.

Alternatives like getting lost in a soft, giving woman who made him want to believe in love—a concept, he reminded himself, that he'd learned early on was an illusion as transient and as elusive as time.

No matter how diligently he tried to reanchor himself in proven realities, the unproven ones wouldn't let him alone.

Restless, unsettled, he rose and prowled the bedroom. It didn't dawn on him for a while that he was looking for something. What, he didn't know. Answers maybe. To what made Carmen tick. Missing pieces that might have clued him in to the fact that she had a son.

Finding none, he stared at a single picture on her dresser that he hadn't noticed from his vantage point on her bed. It was a recent shot of the two of them together. Nothing formal, just a Polaroid someone had taken that she'd tucked into a small frame. And, he realized as he looked around him, it was the only picture of Juan in the entire house. No baby pictures on the walls, nothing to chronicle a history.

Puzzled, he wandered back into the extra bedroom that he knew accommodated Rico and confirmed his first impression. It wasn't really decorated with a little boy in mind.

Something wasn't ringing true. Without tipping his hand—he wasn't yet ready to do that—he decided he needed some answers. He picked up the phone and made another call. After a short but informative chat with Dallas, he had enough of an explanation to understand what was going on. What he didn't understand was how he felt about it.

Pensive, he stared out the living-room window, out to the street five stories below, which rumbled with the sounds of the city and the poverty of the projects only a block or two away.

He was on foreign turf. Totally out of his element. He was as much of a stranger in Carmen's world as she would be in his. He was as much in the dark about her motivations as she was to his identity. Yet as much as he knew he should be fighting it, he was becoming more deeply embroiled in her life. A life that was light-years away from his in terms of culture, economics, attitudes.

He'd never had to wonder where his next meal was coming from. She had.

He'd never had to agonize over meeting basic expenses such as rent and utilities. She clearly had.

He'd never rolled up his shirt sleeves, dug into the decay, and tried to make a difference one-on-one in another person's life. She had.

And, while under his leadership Prince Enterprises was noted for its generosity with charitable contributions, he found himself bucking both the humility and the shame of being a "have" when the world was filled with so many "have-nots".

How, he asked himself, had he managed to become involved with a woman who turned her back on her own needs for the sake of helping others? A woman who made him question his motives and feel defensive about a wealth he'd worked like hell to accumulate?

The most troubling questions he didn't have answers for either. When had he come to care about what she thought, how she would get by when he was gone, and how, when the time came to leave her, he was going to find the strength to walk away?

FIVE

Logan waited in pensive silence until Carmen and Juan had returned from the museum. Seeing them together, the way they loved each other, made him realize that walking away wouldn't be as simple as logic dictated. It might have been simpler if he hadn't made that last phone call to Dallas.

Dallas had filled him in while Logan was still trying to recover from the idea of Carmen with a child. As it turned out, he shouldn't have wasted the time. While Dallas couldn't provide all the details, he'd related enough information to clarify that this child, who had called Carmen Mom, wasn't her child at all.

Juan wasn't her son, but clearly she loved him as if he were. And Juan loved her as if she were his mother. The bond between them ran as deep and as true as common blood.

Grim-faced, Logan watched Juan, his dark head huddled over the game board he'd spread out across the kitchen table. As his gaze strayed slowly from Juan to Carmen, he reminded himself that he was a man who'd spent his life vigilantly dodging emotional involvement. For thirty-six years he'd been successful. For thirty-six years the self-imposed isolation had suited his purposes.

So he didn't fully understand why their commitment to each other affected him so. He only knew that it did. Profoundly. In the short span of a few days, he'd become as mired in Carmen's life as if he'd stepped in quicksand. That fast, that unsuspectingly, he'd begun to care. Soon he'd be in neck-deep.

An expectant look from Juan nudged him back to the business at hand. "My move?" he asked slowly and distinctly.

Juan grinned and nodded.

He'd been eager to play Chutes and Ladders the moment Carmen had brought him back from the museum. Carmen had been firm. She'd insisted Juan rest while she prepared dinner but promised him that if he did, he could get the game out right after the dishes were done.

The boy hadn't wasted any time. As soon as the last dishes were put away, he'd set things up and issued Logan a challenge.

Aware that Carmen was watching them, sensing Juan's confidence was at stake, Logan fussed idly with the game-box lid, covertly scanning the directions so he'd have an idea as to how to play.

Then he made the mistake of glancing up across

the kitchen table. Carmen was leaning against the counter, her eyes misty.

She was too much sometimes. Too much woman. Too much temptation. Right now she was much too proud and happy. He steeled himself against the pleasure he felt at seeing her that way. He didn't want her looking at him like he was responsible for some of that happiness. Yet it was apparent she felt he was. Her smile said a silent thank-you for taking a little time with Juan.

He slumped back in the chair, scowling. Why couldn't she have been a woman who would have been happy with diamonds? Diamonds would have been simple. He could give her diamonds. He understood a woman who was taken in by their allure. He didn't understand *this* woman or why a gift of diamonds would never bring the sparkle to her eyes that was shining in them now.

She dazzled him. She dazed him. She humbled him.

He clenched his jaw and closed his eyes, feeling like a fraud. He felt a lot of other things too. Pride in her. Affection for Juan. In spite of the fact that he couldn't rightfully claim ownership of any of those feelings, in spite of the fact that he'd been fighting them tooth and nail, he'd still become caught up in them.

He didn't belong in their lives, so what happened after he left them shouldn't matter. Yet it did. He was afraid for Carmen. Afraid it would prove too costly for her to invest all this emotion in a child who wasn't even her own. He was afraid for Juan.

He should have been afraid for himself. He was the one who was in beyond his depth.

A small hand on his arm recalled him to the game. He spun the dial then moved his little plastic person along the winding path on the game board. Juan broke into another broad grin then took his own turn.

"He's come a long way in a few short months, hasn't he?"

Even before he looked up, Logan knew that the pride and love projected in Carmen's voice had also touched her face.

"I wasn't sure I'd ever see him like this," she continued. "Inquisitive. Communicating. Happy. He is happy, don't you think?"

Juan bounced a couple of times in his chair and made a muffled, mewling sound of delight when his little red man pulled ahead of Logan's blue one.

Logan grinned in spite of his determination to maintain a fighting distance from emotions that were threatening to turn his insides to mush. "Wouldn't you be happy if you were beating the pants off someone who's not only older but supposedly wiser than you?"

She smiled . . . a smile that slowly faded as a troubling thought dimmed it. "When I think back to the day I first saw him at the clinic, I can't believe he's the same little boy."

It was the opening he'd been both waiting for

and dreading. Dallas's account of the relationship had been informative, though sketchy, because of the limited time they had to talk. This was Logan's chance to have Carmen fill in the blanks. This was his chance to become more deeply embroiled when he should be struggling like hell to break free.

"How long has it been now?" he asked, knowing as he did so the gravity of the error he was making.

"Six months, yesterday." She shivered and hugged her arms around her waist as if trying to ward off an ugly memory.

"He was so lost. I can still see his eyes. Vacant. Wary. No."

She stopped, closed her eyes, and corrected herself. "Not wary. Void." She opened her eyes. "I remember thinking then that I wish he *had* been wary. At least it would have indicated he had some fight in him. He had withdrawn so far into himself, I didn't think he'd ever come back."

She looked from Juan to Logan. "I'm glad you didn't see him then."

"Tell me about it." The tone of his voice gave away the tension he felt.

When she lowered her lashes and looked away, he pressed her, sensing she needed to talk about it even though it might be difficult for her.

"Tell me, Carmen. Rico's told me bits and pieces," he lied, knowing he was pushing his luck. "I'd like to see the whole picture. And I think," he added intuitively, "that maybe you need to talk about it."

She turned her back on him, drew a deep breath then started rummaging around in the cupboard. Slowly, methodically, she set about popping popcorn as she reluctantly began relating Juan's story.

"Juan's mother was little more than a child herself when he was born. She was alone and didn't know how to take care of herself, let alone a child like Juan—and the three other babies that came in rapid succession. Ignorant, alone, totally at a loss as to how to deal with him, she'd leave him in a crib or a bed all day, never talking to him, feeding him when she thought about it, but for the most part ignoring his existence and the reminder of her own failures and imperfections and hopelessness."

Tension, anger, outrage. They all swelled inside him as he listened. He tried to feel some of the compassion he heard in Carmen's voice for Juan's mother, but all he could see was the pain she had inflicted on the child.

He knew about neglect. He supposed that if it were reduced to black and white, he'd even suffered it as a child. But his experiences were nothing compared to the neglect coupled with ignorance and poverty that Juan had endured. He'd wanted only for affection. Juan and thousands of children like him wanted for something as basic as food and health care and the assurance of a roof over their heads.

"It was an accident that a neighbor found him that day."

He snapped himself back to the sound of Carmen's voice. Difficult as it was, he wanted to hear everything she was telling him.

"His mother had left him alone. It wasn't an isolated occurrence. What was different about this time was that while she was gone, someone broke into the apartment. When they found nothing worth stealing, they left the apartment door wide open and moved on. A neighbor happened to walk by and see the open door. When she called out and no one answered, she peeked inside and saw Juan. Alone. Filthy. Hungry. Silently staring and rocking."

She stopped, swallowed, and began again. "Anyway, fortunately for Juan, she didn't think about the possible consequences. She became involved. She picked him up and brought him to the clinic. I was working the night shift when she brought him in."

She walked over to the table and touching her hands to Juan's shoulders, leaned over and gave him a hug. Juan stretched his arms over his head, wrapped them around her neck, and hugged her back. As soon as he returned her quick, nuzzling kiss, his attention shot back to the game.

"Do you know how special that is?" she asked with a watery smile. "That spontaneous reaction? And then the quick dismissal? At one point he didn't react to affection at all. When he finally did, he tried to gorge himself on it. He clung and demanded and acted out violently if he didn't feel he was getting his share of hugs. Now he accepts them, gives them back, and then forgets about it. It shows that he feels entitled.

He's feeling more and more secure. And it means he trusts me to be here for him."

"And you hold that trust sacred," Logan said, knowing, before she confirmed his statement, just how sacred.

"I was a little worried about the way he reacted to you, though."

"You mean the clinging-vine routine?"

She nodded and Logan knew that while she was remembering Juan's insistent grip on his legs, she was also remembering the circumstances. So was he. He'd been wet from the shower, barely hanging on to a towel that covered little and had threatened to reveal more than either of them had been prepared to deal with.

"The more I think about it, though," she said, averting her gaze from the path it had taken to his chest before straying to his mouth again, "I think it's okay. He hadn't seen you for a while. It was an affirmation on his part that you were okay in spite of your bruises.

"How are you feeling, by the way? If he's wearing you out—"

Logan cut her off with a dismissive wave of his hand. "I'm fine. I'm okay," he amended when she scowled at him. "I feel a damn site better than I did yesterday. Or for that matter than I did this morning."

This morning.

This morning in her bed.

They stared at each other. The taste of morning desire, the glide of his hands across her supple flesh, the erotic brush of lips and tongues—the memories of their aborted lovemaking lingered in the room like an alluring fragrance. Tantalizing, seductive, demanding attention.

They had both felt the flame when they'd come together. Spontaneous combustion. Sizzling heat.

He wanted to feel the fire again. He could see in her dark, telling eyes that she wanted it too. He could also see she was fighting the lure.

"It's quite amazing, really," she said, her voice laden with a telltale huskiness.

She was amazing. The way she looked, the way she cared, the way she turned him inside out with the guileless drop of her lashes.

He forced himself to respond to her words. "What's amazing?"

Very deliberately she avoided looking at him. "How Juan took to you from the beginning."

Logan shifted uncomfortably in his chair. More complications. He was pretending to be someone he wasn't. They were both pretending they hadn't been affected by everything that had happened between them the past forty-eight hours. And to top it off, he was beginning to feel royally ticked that Dallas not only had her heart, but Juan's as well.

Juan had taken to Dallas, not to him. It was small consolation to know that at least he wasn't maligning that affection.

Her soft voice dragged him back to the here and now.

"As little as three months ago, he fought any show of emotion like a tiger. But you should have seen him at the museum this afternoon. Once, those beautiful eyes of his had been bleak with the despair of isolation. Today they were round and bright with excitement."

She laughed softly. The gentle sound made Logan's chest ache with emotion.

"I had to struggle to keep up with him," she said happily as she filled three small bowls with popcorn. "He wanted so badly to communicate that his little fingers were flying like crazy. His signing vocabulary is still pretty limited but *wow* popped up regularly. I felt every *wow* full measure."

Logan was feeling a *wow* or two himself. And the reason for and dangers of those feelings had ceased to amaze him. A week ago he wouldn't have taken the time or invested any interest in the state of the human condition. Corporate structure, interest rates, and the stock market were the very air he breathed. A week from now he'd be back in that atmosphere. When he compared it with the reality Carmen and Juan had injected in his life, the prospect seemed stifling and stale.

When he contemplated the possibility of leaving Carmen behind—He cut that thought short. Possibility? The word implied he had an option. No options were open on that front. He *would* leave her behind.

He would leave them both. The reality weighed heavy and dark.

"When did you learn to sign?" he asked her softly.

She walked to the table, a bowl of popcorn in each hand. Logan shifted to give her access as she leaned between him and Juan to set the bowls on the table. He touched a hand lightly to her waist as he made room. It was a careless gesture on his part. Careless and uncalculated. And dangerous. He was totally unprepared for the bonfire that ignited at the exact spot where his hand settled and lingered.

A glittering awareness told him she felt the heat too. The fire spread between them, aided by the dry tinder left over from memories of the night with her in his arms and of this morning when he'd almost made love to her.

Had it only been this morning? It seemed a lifetime had passed since he'd held her. Since he'd tasted her and wanted her. Since he'd hurt her and sent her away.

Slowly he let his hand drop.

Just as slowly she moved back from the table.

"When did I learn to sign?" she repeated, busying herself at the sink, working overhard at pretending she hadn't been affected by his touch and by the look that had passed between them. "I'm still learning. It's not really that difficult. It only takes practice. Hearing-impaired children who are raised in a normal, loving environment usually begin signing as two-year-olds." She smiled sadly at Juan. "Juan never had that opportunity. He's a fast study, though, now that he knows there's more to life than endless silence and cracked, colorless walls."

As she talked Logan forced himself to swallow back a feeling of outrage that threatened to strangle him. Outrage at Juan's biological mother for the abuse and neglect she'd inflicted on this child, and outrage at a society that had closed its eyes to his suffering.

"How did this happen? Why didn't someone know about him? Hadn't she ever taken him to a doctor, for God's sake?" He steeled himself to look away from Carmen, not wanting her to see the rage that must surely be written in the taut muscles of his face. "Didn't she have any family or a social worker or someone to make sure she took care of him?"

He must have pounded his fist on the table. He didn't remember doing it, but Juan's wide black eyes flashed to his with wary curiosity.

He forced a smile of reassurance and was rewarded with a tentative grin. "My move?" he asked hopefully.

Juan nodded in confirmation.

"Alone in a city of strangers," Carmen commented.

Her quiet statement told Logan a great deal.

When he closed his eyes and shook his head, she continued. "We searched all the hospitals and found no records of any kind. His mother's not talking, but we suspect it was a home birth. And we're not taking any chances. Poor Juan has had to endure the complete gamut of vaccinations, just to be sure."

"What about the other children? What's happened to them?"

"Juan's brother and his two sisters have been placed in a single foster home. It's a temporary fix until a decision can be made as to what will best serve their interests."

"How is it that you ended up with Juan?"

She joined them at the table, attempting for the boy's sake to be intrigued with the action on the game board. "I didn't."

She looked up and shrugged when he frowned. "I wanted him. I still do. But I'm not family. In the eyes of the court, I'm only an interested party, even though I've gone as far as applying for and being approved for a foster-parent license. But he needs specialized care right now. Care that I can't give him. Not yet. That's why he's living at the group home. If he keeps improving, though, there's a chance I can have him with me soon."

"He's with you now," he said quietly. "Why? How?"

"Special-needs children are harder to place than quote normal, healthy children. I expressed an interest. Given the shortage of other options, my interest was enough. The group home he's in is geared to his needs. The only thing it can't provide is long-term stability. A long-term family setting. My willingness to bring him home with me for short visits is in keeping with their case plan. It's important that he's exposed to a family setting—or something reasonably close to it. I fall in the category of 'reasonably close.' "

"And when the time comes and he's ready for that long-term family setting," he began, feeling an uncomfortable sense of unease creeping up on him, "are you assured you'll get to have him then?"

She clasped her hands on the table and stared at them. Logan stared at them, too, aware of how tightly she gripped her slim fingers together.

"No guarantees," she said without looking up at him. "There is his mother to consider."

"His mother?" He couldn't keep the disgust from his tone. "What does she have to say about it after what she's done? What rights could she possibly have?"

"She has all the rights."

He could see that she was struggling with that inequity even as she tried to explain it.

"She has the parental rights—at least she does until the courts say otherwise. We won't know for some time if those rights will eventually be taken away."

Logan had to work at unclenching his jaw. "What about *his* rights?" he demanded, nodding in Juan's direction. "After what she's done to him, I can't believe any judge would consider that putting him back with her would be an option."

She drew a deep breath. "After several months of

counseling, she'll be offered an opportunity to prove she's got her act together."

Incredulous, he stared at her. "You mean, she really could get him back?"

She looked grim. "It's a definite possibility."

"This is crazy. Why would she even want him? She didn't take care of him when she had him. I would think she'd be glad to be relieved of the burden."

"It's more a question of economics."

Some of the bitterness he sensed she'd been fighting had finally crept into her voice.

"I don't follow."

She sighed in resignation. "As a single mother with children who are dependent on her for their care, she's eligible for a monthly payment from the state to help her meet their needs. If she doesn't have the children with her, she doesn't get the money."

"But if she was receiving the money and still wasn't providing for them, what makes you think anything will change?"

"Maybe she didn't know how," she said generously.

He slumped back in his chair. "I don't understand how you can defend her."

"I'm not defending her. I'm trying to prepare myself for all the possibilities. Quite frankly the chances of Juan returning to his mother are much greater than the court placing him with me."

Logan didn't much care for the possibilities, especially if it meant she could end up losing Juan . . .

which would mean Juan, too, would be a big loser.

He looked from Juan to Carmen and decided there was no way in hell he was going to let that happen. He might have to leave them, but that didn't mean he couldn't do something to help them. He drew a deep breath, determined, before he left, to get the full picture. Determined he *would* help them.

And when she rose and started making noises about it being time for Juan to go to bed, he decided something else. It was time to tell her the truth about himself.

Carmen smoothed the sheet over Juan's little body then leaned to press a soft kiss on his cheek. She lingered awhile at the door, watching him, wishing she didn't have to take him back tomorrow. This visit was far too brief.

While his initial progress had been slow, he had really blossomed during the past few months. The breakthroughs the counselors had accomplished had been phenomenal. Juan's efforts to close himself off from the world by refusing to sign had been completely thwarted. For the first time she could see the possibility of a happy, healthy future for him.

Mom. She hugged herself, remembering. He'd called her Mom. Her eyes filled and she felt warm all over just thinking about it. She should have corrected him. She hadn't been able to find it in her heart to do so.

After a last, lingering look, she turned off the light and slipped out of the bedroom. She found Johnny on the sofa in the living room. A deep scowl on his face, he stared in silence, unaware that she was there.

She leaned against the door frame, watching him. Without asking, she knew he was thinking about Juan and the precarious circumstances under which she was able to have him with her.

Life, she'd found out, was precarious. And Johnny Dallas, a man she'd thought she'd known, was a major contributor to the sense of loss she felt where her own sense of equilibrium was concerned.

He was becoming such an enigma to her. He'd been much easier to deal with when she'd had him pigeonholed as nothing more than a good-time Charlie with a pretty face. Just another heartbreak with a Texas-size grin.

But now she had this new side of him to cope with. This caring, concerned side that was more compelling than the flirt had ever been.

She didn't understand this unprecedented interest he had taken in Juan's future. While he'd always been kind to Juan, the extent of his involvement had been limited to a big smile, a pat on the head, and the gift of a candy bar.

In many ways since the beating, he seemed so very different from the man she'd thought she'd known. So different, she was beginning to wonder if she'd ever really known him at all. And she was feeling guilty for selling him short.

She pushed away from the door and walked toward him, trying to block the memory of this morning. She wanted to get past the physical, beyond the humiliation, and find out what this man was really all about.

She sat down beside him. Tucking her feet under her, she draped an arm over the sofa's back.

"Who are you?" she asked very softly

After a long, guarded silence, he looked at her.

The room was very quiet, she thought, listening to the tick of the quartz clock on the wall, hearing the muffled sound of an apartment door opening and closing outside in the hallway. The rush of her blood pounded in her ears.

"Who are you really?" she repeated. "I thought I knew. Lately, though, I'm not so sure. The Johnny Dallas I believed I knew was quick with that winning grin and quick to help, but he was even quicker to run when a situation started reeking of complications or involvement."

He looked away, but not before she saw an expression of wrenching agony on his face.

She studied his profile, wondering what was going on in his head that would cause such a look. Shaking off a niggling sense that she should be wary of the Pandora's box she was opening, she probed further.

"The Johnny I knew would never have asked the questions you asked tonight. He wouldn't have asked because he wouldn't have wanted to know the answers. If he knew the answers, he might have to get involved in finding better ones."

Logan's tension was palpable, crowding into the room like another presence.

"The Johnny I knew," she began again, then hesitated when her heartbeat warned her against it. "The Johnny I knew . . . would never have stopped what he'd started this morning. Not for my sake."

The words were out. Like her heartbeat, the memories thrummed through her body, alive, electric. Was he, too, thinking of the way he'd coaxed her into bed last night, then gently held her? Was he thinking of the heat and sensations they'd shared in the dreamy haze of morning?

She hadn't been able to stop thinking about it. Or about the rejection that had followed. As painful as it had been at the time, she suspected that he'd told her the truth when he'd said he desired her, but that he hadn't wanted to hurt her.

She desired him too. But there was more than desire involved here. She cared about him or she couldn't have acted the way she had when he'd kissed her. Yes, she responded to him on a level as elemental as sexual attraction. But she hadn't been ready to compromise herself merely for the sake of satisfying a demand as basic as lust.

She'd reacted to so much more. He'd touched her and she'd been lost. Lost and at the same time found and recognized for what she was. A woman.

A desirable woman. A woman making love with a man whose explicit sexuality exuded from every pore of his body, but whose ability to care and to take care was shielded behind a don't-give-a-damn front. She'd reacted to that hidden side of him. The side she wanted to get to know better.

"What made you stop, Johnny?" she asked softly, still uncertain if she regretted that he had. Uncertain if he regretted it too.

He swallowed hard. "It just wasn't a good idea," he said finally, restating the explanation he'd given her this morning.

She didn't buy it. Not anymore. "Not a good idea for me or you?"

His gaze shot to hers. A gaze full of heat and sparks and frustration.

He didn't answer her, but in his eyes, in the tense set of his jaw, he told her what she needed to know. He'd wanted her then. He wanted her now. As hard and uncompromising as he seemed at the moment, she felt his need. And his vulnerability. Neither was as minimal or as transient as he'd like everyone to believe.

Her hand trembled as she reached out, touching her fingers to his hair. "The Johnny I thought I knew would have taken what he wanted, good idea or not. He'd have said the hell with the consequences. The hell with who got hurt."

He snagged her wrist, wrenching her hand away. "Carmen, you're treading on dangerous ground."

His grip was hard and tight, his intensity bordering on violent, a self-directed violence bred of a dark, aching despair that touched her heart and spoke to her of secrets and desperation and desire.

He wouldn't hurt her. To show him she knew that, she pressed him. "Dangerous? Dangerous for me, Johnny?"

The strong fingers wrapped around her wrist tightened then slowly let go. "You're looking for something that's not there," he said. "Don't bother. You'll only be disappointed in what you find."

The conviction in his tone shook her, but it didn't sway her. "Too late. I've already looked. And I'm not disappointed in what I see."

He made a sound that would have passed for a laugh if it hadn't been woven so heavily with cynicism. "And what, exactly, is it that you think you see in me?"

He sounded so angry . . . and so weary. She watched the tension mount on his face and wondered why she'd ever thought she'd known him. Three months wasn't much time to take the measure of a man. And in those three months she'd seen him only fleetingly. He was either breezing in or breezing out, always on his way to bigger things, wilder women.

She was beginning to wonder if she'd been so blinded by and wary of his bad-boy grin and his don't-give-a-damn swagger, she hadn't seen past the sex appeal to the caring man inside. Maybe her ego had been so bruised by his big-brother act and his roving eye that she missed the depth he'd hidden behind a macho front.

She saw it now. She even thought she might under-stand it now. She studied his face, the strong bones and sculpted angles that made him such an attractive man. She studied the bruises and cuts that she knew still caused him pain. Yet she got the distinct impression that the prospect of Juan being returned to his mother's care hurt him far more than any of his physical injuries.

"I think I see a man who cares more about people than he wants to admit," she said, suddenly sure of her answer.

He closed his eyes and shook his head. "I can't afford to care."

His conviction was so complete that she hurt for him. "And yet you do. You do care. You're involved, yet for some reason you don't want to be. Why is that, Johnny? Is the price really so high?"

This brooding, troubled side of him puzzled her. It was a side she'd seen in the middle of the night when he was hurting. A side she wanted to reach out to now, to wrap herself around and shelter as she sheltered Juan.

"Johnny—"

He shot off the sofa.

All restless energy and edgy frustration, he paced the length of the room, then whirled to face her. Hands on his hips, he squared off, his expression combative and dark.

"You want to know who I am?" he demanded. "You want to know who Johnny Dallas really is? Well, you're asking the wrong man."

The depth of his anger startled her. He was reacting with far more agitation than circumstances warranted. And though she didn't like to admit it, he was beginning to scare her.

Something wasn't right here. For the first time it occurred to her that the blows he'd taken to his head could be responsible for his personality change.

Head trauma. The words echoed in her mind like an indictment. She was a nurse. She should have seen the signs. She should have gotten him to a doctor.

"Dallas, where the hell are you?" he muttered as he stalked across the room then leaned back against the door, looking haggard and caged—the strike of a match away from combustion.

"Johnny . . . maybe . . ." She hesitated, rose, and went to him. "Maybe you should lie down for a while."

He sighed wearily and met her concerned gaze.

"And maybe it's time for the truth."

"The truth?"

Reacting to her troubled frown, he grasped her arm and led her back to the sofa. "Carmen, sit down. We've got to talk."

At a loss as to how to read the situation, she did as he asked, wishing she were as calm as she wanted him to think she was. She wasn't fooling either one of them. When a knock sounded at the door, she jumped as if she'd been shot.

Whoever it was, she didn't want to deal with him or her now. She wanted to concentrate on Johnny.

But Johnny seemed to be expecting someone. He rose, gave her a long, searching look, then walked to the door. Pausing with his hand on the knob, he turned back to her. "I want you to know . . . no matter what you think of me when this is over . . . it was never my intent to hurt you."

A very real sense of foreboding swamped her. "Johnny, what's going on?"

A closed look came over his face. Then he turned and opened the door.

"What the hell took you so long?" he muttered, then stood aside for the man who filled up the doorway—a man Carmen recognized on sight by the flash of his blue eyes and his don't-give-a-damn grin.

On unsteady legs, she rose from the sofa as Johnny Dallas sauntered into the room.

"Hey, Carmen. How's it going?"

She felt the blood drain from her face as she stared from one ruggedly handsome face to the other. From one broad, flashing grin to one dark, sullen scowl.

From one heartbreak to another.

Johnny's grin quickly changed to a look of discomfort when he saw her deathly pallor. "Oh, man. He didn't tell you, did he? He called and said to come over. I swear, Carmen, I never would have come if I'd known he hadn't told you first."

In stunned silence, she looked from Johnny Dallas to the man she'd wanted him to be.

No. He hadn't told her. He hadn't told her, but she realized now that she should have known. Deep down she suspected she *had* known. She simply hadn't wanted to admit it.

She hadn't wanted to know that the man who had held her in the night, the man who had made her feel like a woman, the man who had stolen her trust was also the man who had betrayed her.

SIX

Logan gazed disinterestedly across the gleaming walnut surface of the boardroom table. The board members' heated discussion droned on around him like the irritating wheeze of a poorly oiled machine.

Tuning out the conversation, he rose, walked to the window, and stared at the Transco Tower. The obelisk-shaped structure rose seventy stories above the other corporate and residential buildings making up the Galleria Area. He shifted his gaze to the city streets below; they were bustling with activity.

Heat shimmered on the pavement in waves as an arid August wind sent dust and debris swirling. In the midst of a crowd of people, he spotted a dark-haired woman holding the hand of a little dark-haired boy. He superimposed the image of another woman, another child.

"Logan?"

Ben's voice broke through the void he'd tried to create, the one he'd blended into too often in the past two weeks to suit either Ben or the other board members.

Ben's footsteps were silent on the plush gray carpet. "Logan," he said softly as he walked up behind him. "We need your input to tie up this offer."

Logan turned in stony silence. He recognized the look on Ben's face. He'd seen it often lately. Behind a facade of unruffled control, Ben was frazzled down to his imported Italian loafers.

"Just handle it," Logan said quietly. He turned back to the window. "Then get them out of here."

Ben tensed, collected himself, and faced the group.

"Gentlemen," Logan heard him say with a cheerfulness that betrayed none of his underlying irritation, "the time seems to have gotten away from us. I know you'll understand that we need to adjourn for today. Mr. Prince has prior commitments."

Peripherally aware of a round of grumbled protests, Logan listened with half an ear to the sounds of the room clearing. When the double brass doors shut with a muffled click behind the last board member, he turned to face Ben.

Frustration spurred a surly impatience totally foreign to Ben's nature. Logan felt a twinge of guilt over causing it. Ben Crenshaw was one of the few men Logan trusted implicitly. They'd met in college and had kept in touch from a distance until ten years ago when Logan had brought him into the company. He'd never regretted the decision.

Ben's diminutive stature and penchant toward

plumpness fooled many into overlooking his business acumen, his Yankee perspective, and sharp mind. All those qualities along with innate integrity made him invaluable as a friend and a business adviser.

He didn't look too friendly at the moment, however. His warm brown eyes, usually dancing with good humor, were snapping with irritation.

"Logan, this has got to stop. You're losing their confidence. If it keeps up, you'll also lose control."

Ben was right. Logan knew it. He just didn't know how he felt about it. At the moment indifference was the best he could muster. It must have shown on his face.

"Dammit, Logan. What's wrong with you?"

Logan thought of a pair of soft Spanish eyes. Eyes he'd last seen two weeks ago. Eyes that had gone from caring to closed in a heartbeat when the truth of his deception had come to light. They haunted him.

He could still see Carmen's face when he'd opened the door to her apartment and Dallas strolled in. She look stunned. Then wounded. Then betrayed.

"I knew trading places with that Dallas character was a bad idea to begin with," Ben mused aloud, dragging Logan's thoughts back to the present. "You haven't been the same since. What happened to you when you were gone, anyway?"

Logan didn't want to think about what had happened to him. He wanted even less to admit it.

"Leave it alone, Ben," he said, picking up a crystal paperweight and absently testing its volume in his palm.

Ben drew a deep breath, closed his eyes, and strove for patience. "It's the woman, isn't it?" he asked finally, as if a light had dawned.

Logan glanced at him, eyes narrowed.

"All those favors you've been calling in trying to make sure she gets custody of that little deaf kid," Ben continued, undaunted by the silent warning. "It wasn't only because you wanted to repay her for taking care of you. You've got a thing for her."

Logan faced the window again. "I said leave it alone."

A lesser man would have backed down. Ben Crenshaw wasn't a lesser man. "Like hell I will. If you think I'm going to stand around and watch while you throw away everything you've worked for because you've got the hots for some little tamale—"

One look from Logan cut him off. One dangerous, you're-treading-on-thin-ice look.

Ben considered him with renewed interest. "So that's the way the wind blows. This one's different."

He walked across the room and settled a hip on the table. "Look, as your business associate, I'm telling you you're committing corporate suicide. As your friend, I'm begging you to get yourself together. It's been two weeks. If she means that much to you . . ." He paused and gave Logan a meaningful look that said he was trying to understand, "Then for God's sake, do something about it. If you want her, go after her."

Logan shifted his shoulders. "That's not a possibility."

"Why?" Ben shot back. "Because she's Hispanic? Because she's not on the preferred list of the country-club set? Because your old man would have a bloody stroke if you brought someone of her background home to meet the family?"

Ben couldn't have been further from the truth. For that reason, his accusations stung. Logan had thought Ben Crenshaw was the one person who knew him. But if that's what Ben wanted to believe about him, let him. He hid his disappointment under a careless shrug.

Ben laughed, but without humor. "Sell it to someone else. I'm not buying. You don't give a damn about her pedigree. You care about her."

Logan faced his friend, feeling more relief than he should have. "Believe what you want, then."

"I'll tell you what I believe," Ben said, ignoring Logan's frown. "I believe you're in deep on this one and you don't trust your feelings to steer you through it. I believe you finally found a woman who was able to crack that cynical reserve you've posted around yourself like no-trespassing signs. You're running scared. You've finally found out you're not immune to what the rest of the human race has been suffering for generations."

"Love has nothing to do with it," Logan stated flatly.

"Oh, were we talking about love?" Ben smiled

slyly. "I'll be damned. And here I thought we were talking about indecision."

Logan clenched his jaw.

"I guess indecision isn't your problem after all. You've shot right past it. You know what you want, Logan. And from the way you've been acting, I think you know what you need."

"What I *don't* need is a budding Cupid in a pin-stripe suit."

Ben laughed. "You need a kick in the ass, if you ask me."

Logan cocked a brow. "I don't remember asking you."

Rising, Ben clasped his hand firmly on Logan's shoulder. "Yeah, well, maybe you should have. The way I see it, it's pig simple, friend. You want her? Go after her. Just do us both a favor and get to it before you take me and Prince Enterprises down with you.

"Take the chance, man," he added meaningfully. "If she's got you tied up in knots this tight, my guess is she must be worth it."

Logan stared out the window long after Ben left. If only it was so simple. That Carmen was worth it wasn't at issue. At issue was the fact that she deserved better than what he had to give her.

Carmen was getting out of the shower when she heard the knock. Slipping quickly into a T-shirt then wriggling into a pair of old jeans, she poked her head into the hall and shouted in the general vicinity of her apartment door. "Hold on. I'm coming."

Slinging her damp towel over her shoulders, she hurried down the hall on bare feet, snapping and zipping her jeans as she crossed the living room.

Gathering her wet hair in one hand, she wrung at its dampness as she reached for the knob. A quick glance at the wall clock had her wondering why Barb, who'd said she'd stop by and give her a lift to work, was so early.

"Sorry I kept you waiting," she said, swinging open the door. "I just got out of the show—" The hand working through her hair stalled midsnag. Her explanation dangled, unfinished, when she saw not Barb Jennings's pixie smile but Logan Prince's electric-blue eyes and dark, sullen scowl. Like an automaton, she slowly lowered the towel.

"You shouldn't open your door like that." His scowl never wavered. "You never know who's going to be waiting on the other side."

Carmen willed her heartbeat to a steady rhythm. "You're right," she said, drawing a calming breath and tightening her grip on the doorknob. "And you make a good point to support that argument."

A ghost of a smile hovered around his mouth, telling her he figured he deserved the barb. Memories made her heart harden against the unexpected gladness she felt seeing him standing there.

She supposed she should be more surprised to see him. Somehow, though, she'd known he would come.

What she hadn't known was how difficult it would be to face him.

Silence, suspended like the time that had passed since he'd left her apartment two weeks before, swelled in the room.

Seeing him again was a cruel reminder of what had happened between them. Both physically and emotionally, everything they'd shared had been predicated on a lie. She'd paid a high price, and was beginning to wonder if she'd ever stop paying.

For many reasons, she shouldn't feel anything but anger. She felt much more. She felt every forbidden longing, every sharp tingle of awareness as his gaze moved along the length of her body, touching her breasts, her hips, her bare feet, and finally her wet, tangled hair.

"May I come in?"

So formal. So pristine and untouchable with his hair perfectly cut and styled. So stiffly elegant in his dark tailored suit and perfectly knotted tie.

He'd recovered from his beating except for a faint, crescent-shaped scar that curled into the corner of his lower lip.

Wounded and bruised, he'd been dangerously handsome. Healthy and healed, he was devastatingly so.

Here was the corporate power player she'd read about. Here was the "Prince" of Prince Enterprises. The one the financial page of the daily paper worshiped for his business savvy. The one the society section drooled over as Houston's own equivalent of royalty. A Texan born and bred, this millionaire bachelor, most notably labeled as cool, aloof, distinctly patrician, made for great copy.

Carmen realized he fit the mold as if it had been made with him in mind. Logan Prince. Any resemblance to the man who had lain naked in her bed, vulnerable and needy, desirable and desired, now seemed like a figment of her imagination.

That man had walked out her door two weeks ago.

That man had faded to a memory.

At least that's what she'd tried to make him. A memory, no matter that her dreams had kept his image too crisply in focus. No matter that every night he drifted through her sleep as vivid as reality, or that every morning when she woke up alone in her bed, the truth of his betrayal cut like the slice of a knife.

To combat the pain, she lifted her chin and drew a deep breath. "What do you want, Mr. Prince?"

He raised a brow.

Could he possibly think she still didn't know who he was? A wildly ecstatic, mildly apologetic Johnny Dallas had filled her in on the grand charade before he'd kissed her good-bye with a gleam in his eye and a ranch near San Antonio on his mind.

She'd seen neither man since that night, neither the good-time drifter nor the brooding corporate raider.

Both men had deceived her. Both men had left her.

Only one had lingered overlong on her mind. The one standing in her door.

"Carmen."

He said her name so tentatively, she realized he must have repeated it.

Startled, she snapped her gaze to his.

"I'd like to come in. Will you let me?"

Pride kept her from turning him away. She could only suffer so much humiliation at his hands, but she wasn't about to let him see how desperately she wanted him to leave—or how desperately she wanted him to stay.

Standing back, she gestured for him to enter, then quickly tucked her hand in her jeans pocket when she realized it was shaking.

"You're a long way from home," she said with as much cool detachment in her voice as she could muster. "But then, I guess you've taken this path before. Funny. I never figured you for a man who'd opt to stroll down memory lane. Or is this more like returning to the scene of the crime?"

That half smile snuck back again. Just a shadow, just a glimpse that touched his mouth but held no humor. "Sarcasm doesn't become you, Carmen. Take it from a true cynic, you should stick with something you know."

"Oh, but I do know. You're the one who taught me."

He looked intently at her. "And for that, I'll always be sorry."

She fought a compelling urge to believe him. So what if he was sorry? So was she. But she was also humiliated, and she'd live with it for a long time.

"If an apology was your reason for coming here," she said stiffly, "you've done your duty."

She needed to get him out of here before she forgot she was supposed to hate him for what he'd done to her. "If there's nothing else, I've really got to get ready for work."

"Carmen, you don't owe me, but I'd like a chance to explain."

He was right. She didn't owe him. And she didn't need to give him that chance. She didn't need to risk hearing his explanation because she didn't want to have a reason to forgive him.

"No need. Johnny already explained about the deal you cut with him. Very inventive. You've made him a happy man."

"I didn't come here to talk about Dallas," he said, advancing a step toward her.

She moved back, telling herself she wasn't running. It simply made sense to keep her distance. After all, except for what she'd read in the papers, she didn't really know anything about him. Not this man. She'd known—she'd *thought* she'd known—another man. Rounding the sofa, feeling safer with its bulk and length between them, she faced him.

"Then please, get on with it. I really do have to get ready for work."

His gaze drifted restlessly around the room before

returning to meet hers. Now that she knew who he was—the wealth he was surrounded by—her Spartan furnishings and the shabbiness of the apartment seemed magnified in her eyes.

She hugged herself, then quickly dropped her arms when she realized the gesture communicated her feeling of defensiveness.

"I want you to know," he began slowly, "that I never intended to use you."

She shrugged. "Yeah, well, I never intended to be used. I guess that makes us even. Live and learn, right? I learned a lot from you, Mr. Prince."

If possible, the look in his eyes grew even darker.

"You'll have difficulty believing this, Carmen, but I learned something from you too."

"You're right. I do have difficulty believing it. Somehow I find it difficult believing anything you have to say."

"Yes, well." A sadly resigned look crossed his face. "I guess I gave you good reason."

Another long, painfully silent moment passed, during which she sensed he was struggling with a desire to defend himself. In the end he must have decided there was no defense for what he'd done.

"Look, I only wanted you to know I'm sorry. For everything. And I'm sorry I bothered you. Bottom line—I wanted to make sure you were okay."

"So now you know. I'm fine."

Why wouldn't she be? Just because she'd been tied in knots since he'd left her? Just because she hadn't slept, or eaten, or been able to forgive her own gullibility didn't mean she wasn't handling things. Just because she couldn't forget the way he'd made her feel when he'd kissed her or couldn't quit wanting and wondering what it would have been like between them didn't mean she wasn't okay.

"Carmen."

Achingly soft, devastatingly caring, his voice all but destroyed her. She gripped the back of the sofa. Damn her eyes. Why did they have to burn and blind her with the misty threat of tears? She blinked hard and looked away.

"Carmen," he repeated on a ragged groan as he walked around the sofa and, with a touch of his hand, tipped her face to his.

She knew she should move. She knew she should run, not walk, as far away from him as she could get. But the piercing intensity of his gaze pinned her. She stood there, searching his face as he grasped her upper arms and pulled her slowly toward him.

His gaze caressed her. His eyes glinted with a fire she recognized as desire. And something else. Something she shouldn't let herself believe, but that moved her far more than his passion.

She saw again his vulnerability, his struggle to deny what he didn't want her to see.

"I haven't been able to stop thinking about you," he whispered.

His admission arrowed to her heart, where it penetrated and burned. Another spark sizzled and flared, then spread deep inside her as his gaze dropped to her mouth and lingered.

"I told myself I wasn't going to do this. I swore I wasn't going to touch you."

She swallowed hard and tried to pull away. "Then don't," she managed to whisper when he held her fast. "Please, don't do this."

But it was too late for begging. They both knew it.

"You think I didn't try to stay away?" The vehemence in his tone revealed the battle he'd waged. "You think I don't know that coming here was a mistake?"

Held captive by his arms, held hostage by his words, she braced her hands against his chest. "Then why? Why did you bother?"

With a fierceness that matched his scowl, he dragged her against him and lowered his head to hers. "This . . ." He whispered against her mouth. "This is why."

And this is what she'd been afraid of . . .

And longed for . . .

And dreamed of. . . .

He took her mouth with a desire that was real and commanding. With a need neither calculated nor controlled. His breath was searing heat and forbidden desire. His kiss was a volatile assault of restless passion, self-directed anger, unrelenting seduction.

She should fight him. He wasn't about to let her. His tongue swept inside her mouth with intent to conquer, not compromise, with a promise to possess not finesse.

He consumed her with his hunger, seduced her with his urgency, asking neither her forgiveness nor her permission, but instead demanding the right.

It was everything wrong. It was everything right. Everything she'd dreamed of. Everything she'd longed for. Nothing she had a right to wish for or cling to.

But his strength was her weakness. His power was her defeat as one strong, seeking hand stole down her back while the other tangled possessively in her hair. His mouth ravaged hers, claiming her, devouring her, until the hands braced against his chest were pulling him close instead of pushing him away.

She sagged against him, sighing in total surrender when he cupped her hips with his large hands and nudged her legs apart with his knee, pressing her intimately against him.

"This . . ." he hissed as he dragged his mouth from hers and trailed a path of fire across her jaw with his lips. "This is what I came for. This . . ." he whispered, possessing her mouth again, "is why I couldn't stay away."

It was the one thing Logan had promised himself he wouldn't do. He hadn't come here to take from her. He hadn't come here out of need.

Like hell he hadn't.

Seeing her again was supposed to put that need to rest, to get her out of his head and out of his life.

But then he'd seen her face. He'd looked into her

soft Spanish eyes, and she'd given him a glimpse of her soul. He'd touched her and suddenly it was his soul, not hers, that was in imminent danger.

She moved like water against him, flowing around him, eddying into him, all fluid grace and liquid fire. Sensual, inviting. She was all he remembered and more than he'd dreamed. Heated velvet, honeyed silk.

And now that he held her in his arms again, he didn't know how he'd ever managed to stay away.

Crushing a handful of her heavy, wet hair in his fist, he tilted her head back until she opened for him again. On a breathy sign, she welcomed his tongue, offering hers, mating with his mouth in an urgent, erotic parody of the love they both ached to be making.

With a groan, he skated his hands down the length of her back, filling his palms with her bottom, pressing her hard against him. Hard into his heat. Hard against his arousal.

He gathered her fully against him, feasting on the sweetness of her mouth. Driven by a desire stronger than any he'd ever known, he reached for the snap of her jeans. When she whimpered but didn't pull away, he walked her backward, pinning her against the wall. She groaned as he tugged her shirt free, tunneled his hands beneath it, and filled his palms with the sweet weight of her breasts.

He couldn't get enough of her. Couldn't get enough of her taste. Couldn't get enough of her texture. And her skin. It burned like fire where he touched her. He skimmed her nipples with his thumbs. Her breath caught on a moan, then rushed out in short, shivery puffs that tasted like honey when he caught them in his mouth.

She was his. In this moment, at this time, she was his, only his, for the taking. And he wanted to take it all. Staking his claim, slaking his need, he pressed his arousal against her hips, damning the barrier of clothing between them. Damning a head-clearing moment of lucidity, that forced him to realize how fragile she was and that if he took her now, she'd hate him for the rest of her life.

Framing her face roughly in his hands, he broke the kiss, then sucked in a deep, controlling breath and willed the blood coursing through his body to cool and slow.

Too fast. He came alive too fast when he was near her, and she became too fragile, too vulnerable in his arms. One look into her dazed brown eyes showed him just how vulnerable.

Pressing his forehead to hers, Logan steadied himself and her with a slow, rhythmic caress of this thumbs against her cheeks.

He knew the moment she came to her senses. Even before the glaze of passion had cleared from her eyes, he felt her body tense with the realization of what had happened.

Her eyes filled with accusation, which quickly turned to shame before she lowered her lashes and looked away.

"No." He caught her jaw in his palm and forced

her to look at him. "Carmen, no. Don't look like that. There's no shame in what's happened. It was honest and real."

"What do you know about honesty?" Her eyes were filled with anguish as she clamped her hands around his wrists and tried to jerk free. "How do you get off even talking about honesty after the way you lied to me?"

"Did that kiss feel like a lie? Did the way I came apart beneath you in your bed that morning feel like a lie?" He pressed his hips intimately against hers. "Does this feel like a lie?"

She closed her eyes and he knew she was remembering. And responding. Aching with need. Wanting to hate him. Hating herself for wanting him.

"Carmen, please, listen to me. I didn't intend for any of this to happen. Not two weeks ago. Not today. And I know you didn't either."

With his palms still cupping her face and her fingers clamped combatively around his wrists, he made her hold his gaze. "It happened. It wasn't your fault. Hell, I'm not even sure it was mine. I swear to God, when I came here, I only wanted to talk to you. I only wanted to see you so I could get you out of my head and get on with my life."

She heaved a long, shaky breath. "So you've seen me. If you really care about me, prove it. Walk out that door and leave me alone."

He clenched his jaw as a gnawing guilt ate at him. Slowly he let her go. "Is that what you want? Is that what you really want?" He watched her eyes, knowing he'd see the truth there.

She nodded, but without much conviction.

"Carmen." Breathing a sigh of relief, he stopped short of touching her again and instead brushed a trailing lock of hair away from her face. "The first time I saw you, I realized something about you. You reveal your emotions through your eyes. And you can't lie. Not to me.

"You don't want me to leave," he insisted, but gently. "You might wish that's what you wanted. And I might wish I could oblige you, but somehow I don't think it's going to work out that way."

Confusion, then a weary shadow of defeat crossed her face. "I don't understand you. I don't understand any of this."

He smiled, weary himself but determined not to fight it any longer. "That makes two of us."

"What do you want from me?" Fire and fury made a triumphant return. "Sex? Is that what this is all about? A curiosity tumble with the little Chicana?"

"You have to know that's not true."

She laughed. A sharp, wounded sound that held little humor and even less belief. "What else could it be? Look at you," she said, pushing him away. In a quick, defensive gesture, she brushed her hair out of her eyes, then tapped her chest with the flat of her palm. "Look at *me*. I'm not even in your ballpark, let alone in your league. In case you hadn't noticed, you're slumming, Mr. Prince. You may not be far from your penthouse in the Galleria in terms of miles, but in social position, you're a continent away."

"If you knew me, you'd know I don't care about any of that."

"But I don't know you, do I?" Her expressive eyes added the painful truth that once she'd thought she'd known him. Once, a lifetime ago.

"That's where you're wrong. You probably know me better than anyone ever has. And because of you, I know things about myself I'd never suspected."

"What, that you're a liar?" Resistance brightened her eyes as she tried desperately to cling to her anger. "That you could play on a person's sympathy to take the best advantage?"

"What I learned is that I'm a man, not a machine. I thought I could take without giving. I learned I can't do that. I wanted to take from you, Carmen. For a while there I even convinced myself that I could. I thought I could play a part and take what wasn't mine, the hell with the fact that you wouldn't be the wiser." He shook his head, reflecting on his own stupidity. "I thought wrong. I didn't want you responding to Dallas. I wanted you responding to me."

"You lied to me," she accused, but her eyes showed her struggle not to be touched by his admission. "You took advantage of me."

"Yes. I did. I'm not proud of it. And I'm sorry that because of it you got hurt. But don't expect me to tell you I'm sorry for what happened between us. I'll never be sorry for that."

Silence, as heavy as her satin black hair, as delicate as her wounded pride, held them hostage in memories, held them captive with anticipation.

"I'll make you a promise you can believe in, Carmen," he said finally. "I'm not backing away from this. I'm not backing away from you, unless you convince me you don't want to be a part of my life."

"A part of your life?" Her eyes were suddenly wild, incredulity replacing her hesitation. "What part could I possibly play in your life?"

He stared at her long and hard. "I don't think I've got that completely figured out yet. I promised you honesty," he added when she looked momentarily bewildered.

"Oh, well." She gave a harsh laugh that relayed her frustration with both him and his statement. "Excuse me for not recognizing it. Tell you what," she went on, her anger evident in the flash of her eyes and the jerk of her chin, "when you figure out exactly where I fit into your plans, be sure and let me know, will you? But don't bother to call. A note will be fine. Which reminds me."

She walked stiffly to a small scared desk nestled in the corner of the room and rummaged around until she found what she was searching for. "I don't want your money, Mr. Prince." She faced him defiantly, extending what he recognized was a check written on a Prince Enterprise account. He should have known when he'd asked Ben two weeks ago to send her the money that she wouldn't spend it.

He looked from the check to her. "That was to reimburse you for your time and the care you gave me."

"I don't care what you call it. It's conscience money and I don't want any part of it."

He scanned the stark apartment before returning his gaze to hers. "Keep the money, Carmen. It doesn't begin to cover what I owe you."

"You're damn right it doesn't." She ripped the check in half and shoved the pieces into his hand. "But what you owe me can't be paid off like a bad debt."

Shouldering around him, she walked to the door and swung it open. "Please leave. I don't want to talk to you anymore. I don't want to see you anymore. And I don't want you coming around here bothering me."

Hugging her arms snugly around her waist, she stared at the floor.

He watched the tense set of her slim shoulders and felt an answering tension build inside him. One thing, and only one, would keep him away from her. "Do you love him?"

Her head came up.

"Dallas," he said, reacting to her frown. "Do you love him?"

"I can't see how that would be any concern of yours."

His heart tried to hammer its way out of his chest as he took a step toward her. "Answer me."

Amid the anger and the righteous indignation, he saw the hesitation before she angled her chin and stood her ground.

"I don't have to answer to you."

He searched her eyes, wanting to see only one answer. It was there, thinly veiled, monumentally important. She didn't love Dallas. She couldn't possibly love him—and respond the way she just had in his arms.

He let out a breath of relief and triumph and tried to figure out how to handle things from here. Bullying her into a verbal admission, however, wasn't going to accomplish a thing.

"You're right," he said, curbing his impatience. "You don't have to answer me. But it seems I have a lot of answering where you're concerned."

He touched a hand to her hair. "This isn't over, Carmen. You need to know that up front. I'll be back."

Tipping up her face, he touched his mouth to hers. His intent was to promise. But her mouth was so soft, her lips so yielding, he lingered, gently arousing, patiently stirring the reluctant fires within her to new life.

He pulled slowly away, brushing his thumb in a tender caress along her cheek. "You'll have to do better than that if you want to convince me to stay away."

After a final searching look, he walked past her and out the door.

SEVEN

"You're pretty quiet today, sweet thing. You wanna talk about it?" Eddie Hernandes hiked a hand on one hip of his baggy white orderly scrubs and leaned a little harder on his mop handle. "Say at my place tonight, a little after nine?"

Carmen made a final notation on a patient's chart before tucking it back into the cart. "Not tonight, Eddie."

Reaching over Carmen's shoulder to replace the chart she'd been working on, Barb Jennings grinned, first at Carmen, then at Eddie. "This guy giving you problems again?"

"I don't wanna give her no problems."

"Yeah, we all know what you *wanna* give her, slick. What we can't figure out is why you can't seem to catch the message that she *don't wanna* what you got."

Another day Carmen would have smiled at Eddie's harmless flirting and Barb's sassy teasing. Today wasn't just another day. Today was the day Logan Prince had shown up at her door, kissed her senseless, and left her questioning both her sanity and her resolve to forget about him.

Undaunted by Barb's smart remarks, Eddie maneuvered his mop around the floor until he was once again in Carmen's direct line of vision. "That right, Carmen? What she says?"

Carmen gave him a friendly smile—the same smile that had probably prompted fast Eddie's proposition in the first place. "You're a nice guy, Eddie. But I'm not looking for a relationship right now, okay?"

"He don' wan no relationship, Carmen," Barb piped up, mimicking Eddie's lazy drawl. "He jus' wanna get you in the sack, right, Eddie?"

"Why you got such a smart mouth on you, Jennings?" he asked good-naturedly.

Barb fluttered her lashes at Eddie. "I guess you bring out the best in me."

"Yeah?" Eddie slicked a straggling hank of long black hair back behind his ear. "Well, maybe *you* wanna come to my apartment tonight and see how good *my* best is," he suggested with a grin full of hopeful innuendo.

Barb gave a snort of laughter. "That's what I like about you, Eddie. Your sense of devotion. And your optimism."

"Do I take that as a yes?"

"In your dreams, Romeo. In the meantime, Masters is looking for you."

"Oh, hell." Eddie glanced nervously over his shoulder as if afraid the head floor nurse would materialize out of thin air.

Eunice Masters had the attitude of a drill sergeant and the tenacity of a pit bull. A hungry one. Everyone, including Eddie, took great pains to stay on her good side.

"What does she want?" he asked worriedly.

"Something about a gross of missing gloves." Barb winked covertly at Carmen. "You been playing doctor again, Eddie?"

Muttering under his breath about needing to check on supplies on the fifth floor, Eddie made for the elevator, glancing furtively over his shoulder for signs of Eunice as he pushed his mop bucket ahead of him.

"You shouldn't tease him so much," Carmen said, working hard at fighting a grin.

"And you shouldn't be so nice to him. It's always getting you into trouble. Besides, Eddie was born to be teased. He'd feel neglected if I didn't give him a hard time at least once every shift."

Barb grabbed another chart and began scribbling. "He was right about one thing, though. You've been awfully quiet all day. You feeling okay, kid?"

Carmen hesitated, then forced a smile. "Sure. I'm fine."

"Ummm." Glancing at Carmen out of the corner of her eye, Barb nodded measuringly. "Like you've been fine for the past few weeks now. You can talk to me, you know."

Barb Jennings and Carmen had begun their tour of duty at Ben Taub Trauma Center together five years before. Barb's background was strictly upper middle class and private school. Despite the difference in their backgrounds, they'd become solid friends and confidantes from word one. Some things, however, Carmen couldn't share. Not even with Barb. Logan Prince and how he had affected her life was one of them.

"I'm okay, really," she insisted, feeling guilty for the lie.

"If you say so."

Barb busied herself checking next week's schedule before ducking behind the nurses' desk to slip off a shoe and massage her aching foot. "Wouldn't have anything to do with that hunk a burning love I saw leaving your apartment when I came to pick you up this morning, would it?" she asked without missing a beat.

Carmen frowned at her clipboard and wrote like crazy.

"Look, I know it's none of my business—"

"You've got that right." Softening her dismissal with a quick, if-you-want-to-stay-my-friend-don't-ask smile, Carmen went back to her chart notations.

Barb, however, whose small stature hid a bullish persistence, was notorious for ignoring Mac-truck-size hints.

"Now we can do this the hard way and I can wheedle the information out of you bit by bit, or you can lay it out in a line. I have a set of very persuasive thumbscrews I keep in my purse for just such occasions. Your choice."

"My choice is to call it a wrap. I'm officially off duty as of"—Carmen glanced at the clock—"forty-five minutes ago. And your line of questioning is officially off limits, *comprende?*"

Barb sighed. Accepting defeat for the moment, she slipped her foot back into her shoe. "And so ends another fun-filled day at Ben Taub. You don't have to be manic-depressive to work here, but it sure helps," she mumbled to no one in particular.

Ben Taub Hospital was Houston's premier trauma center. Both women felt the burn of a ten-hour shift that to them had become routine but to most people would be utter horror. Both women dealt privately and silently with the long-term impact each day's events had on their lives.

Carmen's tension reliever was the volunteer work she did at the free clinic associated with the Casa de Amigos Community Health Center. Barb's favorite tension reliever was food.

"How about a pizza and a pitcher of beer," she suggested hopefully. "Both would taste pretty damn good about now."

"On two conditions," Carmen said, heading down the hall beside her friend. "It's my turn to buy and no probing disguised as small talk."

"Okay," Barb agreed grumpily. "It's a deal. But

I've got to tell you, Sanchez, you're no fun. No fun at all."

It was close to midnight when Carmen let herself into her apartment. Stuffed with pizza, pleasantly mellow from that one last glass of beer Barb had insisted would be good for her, Carmen was still grinning over Barb's snide wit and jaundiced perspective on young Dr. Carrington, whose mission in life was to sleep his way through the entire nursing staff at the trauma center. Barb Jennings's resistance, according to Barb herself, had completely thwarted that mission, however.

Carmen found herself wishing she had that kind of savvy and self-assurance where men were concerned, that playful irreverence that allowed Barb to take men or leave them as long as it suited her own purpose. To enjoy them or torment them, depending on how the mood struck her.

While Barb's free-spirited perspective was enviable in theory, Carmen realized that in fact, it was something she herself could never do.

She couldn't play with anyone's emotions—like Logan Prince had played with hers. His deceit still stung. She wished she could put the hurt behind her. She wished she could forget about him or at the very least think of him with anger instead of with longing.

"Why not wish for the moon?" she grumbled as she headed for her bedroom and stripped off her uniform.

Unfortunately wishing didn't make anything happen. And just as unfortunately, what she truly felt toward Logan Prince made forgetting him impossible.

It wasn't reasonable, it wasn't even smart, but what she wanted more than anything was to believe what he'd told her. She wanted to believe that aside from the physical desire she knew he felt for her that there was something else. Something less fleeting than attraction. Something as substantial as love.

Love. The word wrapped itself snugly around her before an accompanying fear caused her heartbeat to ricochet against her ribs.

"You shouldn't have had that last glass of beer, Sanchez. Will you listen to yourself? Love." She shook her head. "I mean, really. Love? As in loved by Logan Prince? This is a lark for him. A little game. An intriguing diversion."

A knock sounded. She whipped her head toward the door. Every instinct inside her told her who was out there knocking. An unsolicited prickle of excitement at the prospect of it being Logan spurred the sudden acceleration of her heartbeat.

"Make an appointment tomorrow. Neurology. Get that head of yours examined," she muttered under her breath.

Logan Prince couldn't be on the other side of that door. Despite his parting remarks and pretty words, he wouldn't go to such lengths to see her. It was after midnight. Even on a lark, he was not the kind of man who would humble himself with something as common as chasing a woman. Especially not a woman as common as she was.

Besides, from everything she'd read, women chased Logan Prince, not the opposite. Wealthy women. Socially connected women. High-fashion. High-profile.

And those were the women who belonged in his life.

Slipping into a floor-length red satin robe, she berated herself again for the trip-hammer beat of a heart that hadn't given up thinking it might be Logan. Wrapping the robe's belt tightly around her waist, she walked hesitantly to the living room as a knock sounded again.

Barb had been pretty wound up when she'd dropped Carmen off a few minutes ago. It was probably Barb, deciding not to call it a night after all.

She reached for the dead bolt, convinced she'd see Barb's sappy grin, when a low voice penetrated the door.

"Carmen, it's Logan."

She jerked her hand back as if the doorknob were on fire. Her legs weren't as quick to react. She backed slowly away.

When the back of her knees hit the sofa, she sank down onto it, staring in silent denial at the closed door.

"Carmen, open up. I want to talk to you."

Her heart bucked, then lurched into a headlong gallop. Foolish heart. Foolish woman.

Persistent man.

On one level, that pleased her. On another, she realized that without her knowledge, her brain had taken a hike. She'd like to blame her reactions on fatigue. Even on anger. But for all her attempts to call it otherwise, a spade was still a spade no matter how it was disguised. She was thrilled that he'd come back. Thrilled and frightened and at a total loss as to how to defend herself against the feelings he evoked in her.

Until she figured out how to get herself under control, the best defense, she decided, was no response at all. If she ignored him, maybe he'd go away. Logic dictated that if she didn't open up, he'd do just that.

Logan Prince, however, wasn't in a logical mood.

"Carmen, I know you're in there. I saw you come home. A few minutes of your time. That's all I ask."

She drew her knees to her chest and wrapped her arms around them. "You ask too much," she whispered, knowing he couldn't hear her, praying on one hand he'd leave, hoping on the other he'd persist. Not knowing how she would react to either choice he made.

"Come on, Carmen. Either open up, or I'll make such a ruckus out here, you'll wish you had," he warned her after a long silence, and in such a definitive tone, she knew he meant business.

She rose on shaky legs and crossed the room. "Why don't you leave this alone?" she pleaded, pressing her forehead against the door.

"We both know I can't do that."

Praying for strength, she threw the dead bolt.

Logan breathed a sigh of relief when he heard the slide of the bolt and the turn of the latch. It had been a cheap trick, threatening her like that. He felt a twinge of remorse, but it melted to a feeling a righteous justification the moment she opened the door and he saw her standing there.

Red was her color. Satin was her fabric . . . and nearly his undoing.

"Hi," he said, aware of the huskiness of his voice.

"We've played this scene once already today." She watched him with fire in her eyes and a white-knuckled grip on the doorknob. "At the risk of sounding redundant, why are you here?"

Ignoring her cool reception and counting on those telling eyes of hers to reveal her true feelings, he stood his ground. "I told you I'd be back."

She looked so confused. So uncertain. So absolutely lovable.

"You look tired, Carmen. You're working too hard. When was the last time you had a day off?"

"Did you listen to anything I said this morning?" She was trying very hard to stand her ground. But from the slight tremor in her voice, he knew that even she felt herself slipping. "I didn't want to see you then," she continued, working hard at sounding angry, "and just because I let you bully your way in here tonight doesn't mean anything's changed."

But things had changed and they both knew it. Unable to resist, he touched a hand to her cheek, then smiled when she neither flinched nor pulled away.

"I bullied the door open," he said, acknowledging her assessment of his method. "It remains to be seen if that tactic is going to get me inside."

"As if I could stop you."

Turning her back on him, she left the door open in silent, if grudging invitation. Then she walked to the sofa, dropped onto a corner, and tugged her robe tightly around her.

He shut the door behind him as he stepped inside. "Have you wondered why that is? Have you wondered why you couldn't stop me?"

She looked up at him, then away. "Because you're bigger than me."

He grinned, aware as he did so that in spite of the mess he'd made of things between them, since he'd met Carmen Sanchez, he'd been grinning more than he could ever remember. Spontaneous, straight from the gut, just because it felt good grinning.

"Is there a chance it's because of my money?"

"Your money doesn't impress me," she snapped, as if the notion was preposterous.

He grinned again with an odd mixture of self-castigation and relief. He'd known her answer yet felt compelled to test her—a conditioned reflex. The irony, however, wasn't lost on him. He expected her to trust him, but it would seem he needed a little more practice in the trusting game himself.

"That's what's so special about you, Carmen. You're not impressed with my money. You're not intimidated by the implied power."

Snagging a side chair, he pulled it directly in front of her and sat down. He leaned forward, propped his elbows on widespread thighs, and simply enjoyed watching her try to ignore him.

"You want to know the real reason you let me in here tonight?" he asked after a long moment in which she attached a great deal of importance to smoothing the fabric of her robe over her legs.

"By all means. Enlighten me."

"Even though you're trying to deny it—to me and probably to yourself too—the real reason you opened the door is because you really wanted to see me."

The hand smoothing the robe stopped abruptly. "You and Johnny have more in common than I'd thought. His ego needs deflating too. I'm surprised either one of you could fit your heads through my front door."

His grin snuck back, the ease of its recurrence no longer surprising him. While he liked and respected her soft side, this feisty twist was a treat he was beginning to warm up to.

"Carmen, look at me."

When she stubbornly kept her head down, he pried the hand she'd fisted from her lap and folded it between both of his.

"Then listen to me. It's not as if we aren't in this together. It's not as if I don't know that this is probably a huge mistake. The simple truth is that I want to see you. I want to get to know you better. I want you to get to know me. Me," he repeated when she angled her chin at him. "Logan Prince. Not a man you thought was someone else."

She was quiet for a very long time. "You were never like him."

He absorbed her softly spoken statement, unable to decide if she'd paid him a compliment or expressed regret. "I wish I knew what that meant."

"It means I should have known you weren't Johnny."

He squeezed her hand. "Maybe you did know. Maybe you didn't want to admit it."

A denial formed on her lips. That's as far as it got. She couldn't deny it because what he'd said was true. Her inability to dispute him confirmed it and gave him hope.

He looked at her hand, felt both her fragility and her strength, and a little weakness that was his own.

"You need to know something, Carmen. Something I've suspected since I first met you and realized with certainty after I left you this morning. This is new for me too. This business of wanting someone to know me. I've got to tell you that it's a little unsettling. I've never opened myself up like this before. And I never thought that when the time came, it would be to a woman."

Her brow furrowed in confusion.

"There's more to me than money," he went on.

"More than a business machine and a fast track to social position and wealth. Few people have ever bothered to look past that. No woman has ever tried. Until you.

"From the beginning," he continued, choosing his words carefully, "even when you thought I was Dallas, I wanted to know what it would be like to be evaluated by a woman as a man. Only a man, not a free ride, not a trophy."

It had been a difficult admission. Relief flooded him when he saw that she understood what it was costing him.

"I can't tell you how special that feeling was—how special that feeling *is*—for me. I don't want to give it up. Not so soon. Not until I see where this is going."

She swallowed hard and closed her eyes in a vain attempt to hide her indecision. In that moment he knew there was no way in hell he would let her go without a fight.

"What do you say, Carmen? Are you willing to give me a chance? All I'm asking is that you don't say no," he added quickly. "Not to the possibilities. Not to your feelings. Not to us."

He brought her hand to his mouth and placed a lingering kiss there. When he felt her hand tremble, he looked up and found her watching him with a breath-stealing mixture of turmoil, compassion, and longing . . . enough longing to tell him he stood better than a passing chance at winning her.

He'd gambled fortunes with better odds, yet the

stakes paled when pitted against what he stood to lose if he blew it with her.

Instinct told him to take it slow. To let her get used to the idea of thinking of the two of them together.

"Keep thinking about it, Carmen. Tonight, when you're alone, when you're wondering about the way it could be between us, think about the possibilities."

He was thinking of them too. And if he didn't get out of here soon, he'd have no choice but to act on his thoughts.

"I'm going to go now," he said, though it was the last thing he wanted to do. "You're tired. You need some sleep . . . and if I stay any longer, I can't promise I'll be able to let that happen."

Her eyes darkened with shock, then with desire.

"Can I see you tomorrow?"

"I've got to work tomorrow," she said quickly. So quickly he knew she still hadn't accepted the inevitable.

He smiled as he rose, never letting go of her hand. "Haven't you figured out yet that you can't lie to me?"

"Okay," she admitted grumpily, allowing him to tug her to her feet. "So I'm not working. But I promised to spend some time at the clinic."

"Whatever," he said agreeably, and pulled her with him to the door. "But I *will* see you tomorrow. Bank on it."

Her eyes were melting chocolate as she looked

up at him, a part of her wanting to stand firm, a part of her leaning into instead of away from his arms.

"Kiss me good night, Carmen," he said, pulling her gently toward him. "Not because I'm asking you to. But because it feels right. Because you want to kiss me . . . *me*, Logan Prince. Because you know who I am, instead of who I'm not."

Bracing her hands on his chest, she searched his face. "I'm not sure if I'll ever know who you really are."

"Then now is as good a time as any to start finding out."

Folding her snugly against him, he lowered his mouth to hers. With a hesitancy born of her uncertainty, with a willingness that gave way to her longing, she very slowly met him halfway.

Trust was his goal. Tenderness was his approach. But when she relaxed against him and leaned into the kiss, it took every ounce of control he possessed to keep from sweeping her into his arms and carrying her off to bed.

Silken moments later he broke the kiss. On a deep, shaky breath he touched his lips to her hair. "Someday," he whispered, smoothing his hand up and down the length of her braid "I'm going to earn the right to undo this."

He pulled back to look at her face. Her eyes were heavy-lidded, her mouth sweetly parted, expectant, waiting. "Someday I'm going to see your hair spread across my pillow. I'm going to see your body spread across my sheets."

She shivered and closed her eyes at the vividly erotic picture he'd painted.

"Know it, Carmen. Know it's going to happen. And know that when it does, it will be because you want to be there with me."

He kissed her again, deeply, sweetly. "And know this. When it happens, there will be no turning back. Once I finally have you, I don't intend to let you go."

Carmen's hands were shaking as she closed the door. With clumsy fingers, she slid the dead bolt home, turned the latch, then sagged heavily against the door.

For a long time she stood there, recovering from his kiss. When she could move, she walked to her bedroom, slipped out of her robe and into her sleep shirt, and with a frustrated groan flopped to her back on the bed. Flinging her hands above her head, she stared at the cracks spidering the ceiling.

He kissed her with such hunger. He held her with such possession. Above it all, though, he appealed to her with a need that was bone deep, but that he'd let surface with his gruff admissions. She believed him when he'd told her he'd never shared himself with anyone.

And yet he wanted to share himself with her.

He'd told her not only in words, but through his touch, by the restraint he'd shown in not taking her physically when they'd both known she was helpless to resist him, that he would give her time to reach the same conclusion.

She didn't need any more time. A few steamy kisses and she totally lost her head. A few heated looks, the brush of his body against hers, and she'd been ready to throw reason to the wind and get lost in the storm he created.

Perhaps it was her physical response to him that frightened her most of all. She felt helpless when he touched her. She felt wanton and wanting and unabashedly ruled by her body's demands.

Telling herself it was his resemblance to Johnny that kept throwing her off balance wasn't cutting it anymore. The truth was it was the differences, not the similarities that had her mired in doubt.

Johnny Dallas had been the stuff fantasies were made of. His pretty face, his flashing eyes and devil smile all warned a woman away at the same that they compelled her to follow. They also told a woman up front what she'd be risking if she dared play with his brand of fire. He was a "bad boy" committed to his fun. Long-term involvement would never be a part of his plans.

Logan Prince, however, was the stuff that made a woman want to believe in the dream. Despite the fact that he had lied to her, she wanted to believe him when he told her why he hadn't played the charade through to the end.

Yes, it was differences between Logan and Johnny

that made Logan the kind of man she could care about. It was the man Logan Prince really was that made her want to love him.

"Why are you thinking about love again?" she muttered into the silence of the bedroom. "None of it matters anyway."

They came from different worlds. Socially. Financially. She was no match for his sophistication. She no more belonged in his circle than he belonged in hers. Yet here she lay, in her discount-store sheets and her low-rent apartment, wanting to believe in miracles. Wanting to believe that Logan Prince could be her prince who'd tried to hide in the guise of a pauper. That when the story ended, he wouldn't walk away out of boredom, but that he'd ride away into the sunset with her at his side.

"And your next shift at the trauma center will pass without an emergency," she muttered, weary with herself, weary of her wishing.

She had to stop and face facts. No matter how pretty his words, no matter how seductive his kisses, there was no storybook ending in sight.

She rolled to her side and tucked a pillow to her aching breasts as a memory of his large hands holding her, of his hungry mouth seducing her increased the ache. She closed her eyes on a groan, as a deep craving grew inside her.

They would become lovers.

There. She'd admitted it. And in doing so, she'd accepted it.

Restless, yearning for something that couldn't be, she rolled to her other side and thought back to his parting kiss. To his parting words and the way he seemed to crawl inside her head and know the perfect way to touch her in order to leave her melting and wondering. Wondering about love. Wishing it were in the cards.

EIGHT

Since she hadn't been able to sleep anyway—and she had Logan Prince to thank for that—Carmen had risen at five, showered, and caught a bus to Casa de Amigos. Even so early, the twenty-four-hour clinic hadn't been lacking for activity. Besides, whenever a momentary lull settled over the place, there was the endless paperwork that had to be done.

When she headed out the health center's doors at noon, she'd put in six solid hours of volunteer work. And when she hit the heat of the street, the exhaustion of the last couple of days caught up with her—until she looked toward the curb. The fatigue melted away when she saw the man and the boy waiting for her there.

"Juan," she cried in surprised delight, scooping him greedily into her arms when he came barreling toward her.

He snuggled up against her for a sweet, clinging moment, then bouncing with barely leashed energy, tugged her toward the man who had brought him to see her.

Slowly she met Logan's gaze, her tentative smile laced with wonder and thanks.

Wearing khaki chinos, a soft white cotton shirt, and a sexy, I-could-look-at-you-forever expression, he pushed away from the door of a flashy, low-slung, midnight-blue sports car.

"Hi," he said in that gravelly voice that had whispered through her dreams last night and was in part responsible for her restless sleep.

She held his gaze as he walked toward her, unable to conceal her pleasure at seeing him. "Hi, yourself."

Self-assured, without guilt, without guile, without a thought of hesitation, he leaned to her and placed a lingering hello kiss on her mouth. "I told you I'd see you today."

"Yes," she said breathlessly. "You did, didn't you?"

Attempting to slow the wild flutter of her heart, she glanced down at Juan, then braved a look back at Logan. "I guess I'm going to have to start believing you mean what you say."

The smile that unfolded on his ruggedly handsome face was slow and mellow. "And I guess I'm going to have to keep giving you reasons to believe."

Seeing him like this was reason enough, she decided. Sullen and dark, his face was devastatingly appealing. But when he was smiling and relaxed, he took her breath away.

Like now. The look in his eyes told her he recognized that much more than words and a simple hello kiss had just passed between them. It was the beginning of a trust he'd asked for and that she was cautiously giving. It was the crossing of a line. Above all, though, it was a sudden sense of rightness that went a long way toward erasing past wrongs.

"Come on," he said. "Time, as they say, is a-wasting."

With his hand warm and possessive at the small of her back, he leaned down to open the passenger door. "Do you want to go home to change before we get started?"

She shook her head. Her white pants and uniform top would have to do. "Not on your life. I don't want to waste a minute."

Their gazes held for the briefest of moments before she settled in and Juan parked himself happily on her lap.

"How did you arrange this?" she asked over the top of Juan's head as Logan eased behind the wheel.

He shrugged. "What good is money if it doesn't open a few doors."

Though she was grateful, she really didn't want to hear any more. Juan's rare weekend visits were doled out with judicious prudence by the group home counselors. If Logan could increase the time she could spend with Juan, his motives held far more import than his methods.

And his motives, she was beginning to believe as Logan grinned at Juan and gave him a thumbs-up sign, were honest and real.

"How long do we get to keep him?" she asked, realizing as she did that without giving it a second thought, she'd included Logan in their plans.

He realized it, too, though he was tactful enough not to point it out. "Only for the afternoon."

Though she'd been hoping for more, she told him with her smile how precious these few hours would be. And how much his gesture meant to her.

His gaze grew dark with a need she recognized because it matched her own.

"We thought you might be hungry," he said, dragging his attention to the traffic as he shifted into low and pulled out onto the street.

"And what did you think I might be hungry for?" She signed the question for Juan.

He quickly signed back his favorite meal.

She laughed and hugged him hard. "You're right. I couldn't live another single solitary minute without burgers and fries."

After an enthusiastic lunch, it was off to another of Juan's favorite places—the museum again—where Juan shared all his discoveries with Logan.

"He doesn't seem to be confused," Logan said as they walked from one display to another. "About the fact that I'm not Dallas, I mean."

"He's a smart kid," she agreed, remembering Juan's thoughtful looks when she explained how Johnny and Logan looked alike but were not the same men or even brothers. "And even though he liked Johnny, he informs me he likes you too."

A spontaneous grin flashed. "Yeah?"

"Yeah," she confirmed, touched beyond measure by how pleased that information made him and by the importance he gave to Juan's feelings. Touched even more by his follow-up question and the recurrence of that vulnerability he was so hesitant to reveal.

"Have you heard from him?"

"Johnny? No, I haven't heard from him. But I don't expect to." Juan had latched onto her hand and was dragging her off in another direction.

The rest of the day flew by. Too soon the afternoon was over and they'd reluctantly delivered a happily exhausted Juan back to the group home.

Logan was silent beside her as they walked back down the group-home steps to his car. Carmen settled into the passenger seat and, closing her eyes, leaned her head against the headrest as Logan shut the door behind him.

He was quiet for a long time before he touched her shoulder. "It's going to be all right, Carmen. You're not going to lose him."

She wished she could believe he was right. But until it was over and the courts made their decision, she couldn't let herself hope.

She turned to him. "Thank you for today. I needed to see him. And what you did, arranging it, was very special."

"You're very special." He leaned toward her. "And I like very much taking care of your needs."

Very softly, very invitingly, he kissed her, leaving

her weak and wanting and as needy as she'd ever felt.

She all but whimpered when he pulled away and buckled her seat belt.

"And what you need now," he said, reaching for the ignition, "is sleep. You're exhausted."

He made it so easy to lean on him. To count on him. He made it so desirable to believe that life was as simple as they wanted it to be.

But life wasn't simple and neither was it always kind. Her willingness to forget about those truths was telling about her growing feelings for this man. Equal measures of frustration and a wistful kind of hope were threaded through her tired sigh. "I really don't understand you."

He sat back, his hand poised on the gearshift. "What is it that you don't understand?"

"All of this," she said, gesturing with an expansive wave of her hand. "Why you did this today. Why you're here." She turned to look out the window and in a small voice added, "Why you're here with me."

She felt his weight shift as he twisted in the seat. "Where should I be, Carmen?"

His voice was so soft, so caressing, she wanted to lean into it, into him. She shook her head instead and gave a soft, disconcerted laugh.

"Where should you be?" she repeated expansively. "Wherever it is that good little millionaires spend their free time, I suppose. At some exclusive club?

Jetting off to Rio? Yachting off South Padre? I don't know where. Anywhere but here, I guess."

With a gentle pressure of his palm against her cheek, he turned her face to his. "Why can't I just be where I want to be?"

"But that's what I mean. Why wouldn't you *want* to be at any of those other places?"

"I thought we'd covered that last night. I'm here because I'd rather be with you."

She closed her eyes, clinging stubbornly to the notion that he couldn't be for real. "And I'm supposed to believe that?"

"That's the general idea."

"And to be with me, you're willing to spend your free time driving down hot Houston streets, eating hamburgers at a fast-food restaurant, and fighting crowds at a museum?"

He smiled. "I just did it, didn't I?"

"But—"

"But what?"

"I can't believe you enjoyed it."

"There's that word again. I thought we'd gotten past your doubts on that count. Carmen, stop. Think about it. We spent the afternoon together. Did you hear me complain?"

Not only had he not complained, he had actually appeared to be having a good time. "No, but—"

He pressed a thumb gently to her lips, silencing her. "But what, Carmen? Why can't you accept that I want to be with you? Why can't you relax about the way I feel about you and let things take their course?"

Why? Because she wanted too badly to believe he meant exactly what he'd said. Because she wanted too desperately to believe in the two of them together.

"Logan—"

Once again, he cut her off. "No more questions." He reached for the ignition and this time brought the powerful motor to life. "No more doubts. You're tired. Just close your eyes. Enjoy the ride. I'll have you home in an hour."

Actually it was more like forty-five minutes. The only way she knew was because he told her when he gently woke her after pulling to a stop in front of her apartment building. She couldn't believe she'd fallen asleep.

Marginally refreshed, excruciating aware of the man beside her, she slid out of the car. In silence, in a state of suspended anticipation, he walked her to her door. She handed him her key with a trembling hand. It was a blatant invitation to stay. The look on his face, the sudden tensing of his broad shoulders made her heart pound.

Ever so slowly, he crowded her against the door. The dark, musky male scent that had teased at her senses all day seemed suddenly to surround her in a snug and arousing web. His eyes, intense and seeking, searched hers as he flattened his forearms on either side of her head and covered her mouth with his.

It was the first time she'd willingly offered him her mouth without reservation. It was the first time he'd sensed and responded to her open invitation.

Liquid, languid, gloriously carnal yet exquisitely caring, his kiss turned her knees to rubber. He caught her. Never breaking the kiss, he draped her arms around his neck and pinned her firmly against the door with his hips.

His arousal was hot and heavy where it nestled commandingly against the hollow of her belly. His tongue was probing and possessive as he swept inside her mouth to tempt and torment and offer a taste of untold pleasures.

He forced himself to end the kiss. "I swear, Carmen, I was going to leave you untouched at your door. I wasn't going to start this. You're tired. You need to be in bed." He sounded as winded and as aroused as she felt.

"You're right about one thing." Anchoring her hands in his hair, she pulled his head back and nuzzled his jaw with a restless, reckless hunger. "I do need to be in bed."

He swallowed thickly.

"I need to be in bed with you."

He groaned and a fierce, long shudder racked his big body. "And you will be," he promised, "soon."

He looked deep into her eyes and then kissed her once more, thoroughly, aggressively, before he forced himself to pull away. "But not tonight."

Answering the confusion in her eyes with a low,

vivid oath, he bid her a husky, soul-melting good night, and left her.

"Maybe it's like an endurance test," Barb suggested speculatively as she and Carmen ate lunch at a corner table in the cafeteria.

"Right," Carmen agreed, prying open her milk carton and stuffing a straw inside. "And the test results are in. I failed miserably."

Since that day two weeks ago when Logan had appeared at the clinic with Juan in tow, Carmen had seen him almost every day. He'd either been waiting for her after work at the hospital or at the clinic.

Always, he was solicitous and sensitive. Always, he left her at her door with a bone-melting kiss and a promise to see her the next day.

She had stopped trying to keep her involvement with him a secret from Barb. Logan's appearances at the end of each shift pretty well told the tale.

And the tale, as it were, was building in conflict and tension.

"I'd say the man is smitten," Barb concluded, backing the wisdom of what she called her advanced years with a definitive nod of her head.

"I'd say the man is bored with his rich-man toys and is looking for a new experience with someone from the working class," Carmen returned grumpily.

"You know you don't believe that," Barb insisted, forking up a mouthful of something neither of them had been able to identify in the cafeteria line, but only Barb had been adventurous enough to add to her tray. "You'll never get me to believe it either. He's a nice man—emphasis on *man*," she added with a moony-eyed shiver. "And the *man* has got it bad."

"Then why all these advance-and-retreat tactics?"

If frustration were a disease, she'd have died from it. Barb, however, was relishing every event as it unfolded.

"Well, the way I've got it figured," Barb said, "he's giving you the time to come to terms with the idea of the two of you together."

"Come to terms?"

"As in 'How does the little Chicana girl from the projects reconcile the differences between herself and Houston's millionaire heartthrob?' "

And there, in a gold-plated nutshell, was the meat of her dilemma. Carmen slumped back in her chair with a big sigh. "Okay, Carnac, how does she see her way past those differences?"

"By accepting your attraction as a woman and your value. You have a lot to offer a man, Carmen. Face it," she continued meaningfully, *"you're* the one hung up on the superficial differences between you."

"Superficial differences? We're talking heritage here. We're talking vastly differing positions on the social ladder. Barb, the man's very existence is totally intimidating to me."

"The man? The *man*, Carmen? You're not intimidated by the man. You're intimidated by the man's image. And that's *your* problem, not his. There is nothing intimidating about Logan Prince—unless you count the way he looks at you." She waved her hand as if fanning an invisible flame. "I've got to tell you, the way those looks sizzle, when he finally does take you to bed, you are going to be in for one dy-no-mite time."

"And what if that's all there is to this?" Carmen asked, working hard at hiding her insecurity. "What if it's just sex?"

Rolling her eyes, Barb leaned forward, a sympathetic smile on her face. "Sometimes a girl gets lucky and the sex is only as important as the feelings a man and a woman have for each other. That's one thing I haven't heard yet, by the way. What kind of feelings do you have for this guy?"

Carmen looked away.

"Whoa. That bad, huh?"

Carmen shrugged. "There's a fool born every minute and all that."

Though Barb was silent, Carmen was aware that she was watching her. "So," Barb began after a long moment. "When do you see him again? The usual nightly chauffeur service?"

She shook her head. "He had to go out of town on business. But he'll be back tomorrow and wants to take me out to dinner."

"And that upsets you?"

It made her crazy. The proof of how crazy was the state of her nerves by 6:45 the next evening as she dressed for her dinner date with Logan. She was edgy and anxious and wondering not only where the night, but their relationship would go.

Though she'd promised herself she wouldn't, she'd taken great pains with her appearance. And while she'd also told herself she was dressing for herself, she knew she was dressing for him.

The man was manipulative, she decided as she twisted in front of her mirror to get a back view of the dress she'd chosen. He hadn't asked her to wear her hair down, but he'd made it clear that he liked it that way. He hadn't asked her to wear red either, but she knew he liked seeing her in the color.

She'd blown some of her grocery money on the dress and the sinfully sheer satin-and-lace undergarments beneath it. Made of shimmery, elegant silk, the vibrant red long-sleeved shirtwaist was saved from being too simple by the deep V of its wrap bodice and the slim skirt that was slit in front from midcalf to above the knee. A gold jeweled belt buckle and gold hoop earrings were her only accessories. Her cologne was the only reminder of who she was and helped to keep her grounded.

When his knock sounded on her door, however, and her heart lurched in response, she wasn't sure she'd ever feel like she was walking on solid ground again. And when she saw the look in his eyes as she opened the door and he gave her a slow, heated once-over, solid ground ceased to be an issue, because suddenly she wasn't certain if she could even walk.

"The thing about you, Carmen," Logan said after he'd found his voice and was confident he could string more than two words together into some semblance of a coherent thought, "is that just when I think I've seen every facet of you, you show me another."

"Another facet?" she echoed, sounding achingly breathless and touchingly uncertain.

She still didn't know how beautiful she was, he realized as he watched her. She did not accept her desirability. For two solid weeks, and at great cost to his own sanity and self-control, he'd been kissing her senseless, leaving her wanting. The way he wanted. The way he needed. It had all been a prelude to this night.

He'd quit fighting his motives the afternoon he'd spent with her and Juan. He'd quit denying the truth. He was in love with this woman. And if that mind-bending revelation hadn't been enough, he was also determined to make her a part of his life.

For the past two weeks he'd been laying the groundwork to introduce her to that love, to introduce her to his life.

"Another facet, Carmen," he repeated, touching a hand to her glorious mane of hair. "Like a diamond. Every time I look at you, I catch another glittering angle, another play of light, another glimmer of your rare and electrifying beauty."

She blushed.

"I'm embarrassing you."

"Yes," she whispered. "I'm not used to hearing things like that."

"It makes you uncomfortable?" At her sheepish look he smiled. "Then try this on for size. Carmen Sanchez, you are one hot-lookin' mama."

Her unguarded, sexy laugh did amazing things to cut the tension between them.

"Now, *that* I can deal with. And speaking of hot"— she gave his black tux and tie an appreciative once-over—"you're looking pretty impressive yourself."

He bowed his head in acknowledgement. "We aim to please."

She retrieved her purse from the end table and rejoined him at the door. "Then by all means, let's get this show on the road. I didn't dress like this for nothing, you know. I expect to be wined and dined and then some."

With his hand riding possessively on her back, Logan walked her down the hall. The "and then some" played a predominant part in his plans for the evening.

Houston lay at Carmen's feet like a velvet black blanket studded with glittering diamonds. She leaned against the railing on the balcony of Logan's pent-house, breathing in the sultry Texas breeze that played with the clinging silk of her dress. A brass wind chime was singing softly.

Brushing a strand of hair away from her face, she smiled and accepted the glass of wine Logan offered. When he smiled in return, she was taken, as always, by his physical presence. He called her beautiful. Yet if ever an adjective fit, the word fit him. From the rakishly thick wealth of his wheat-colored hair, to the uncompromising lines of his lean, angular face, to the blue of his eyes that tonight were the shade of a slow, seductive flame, he was a beautiful, desirable man.

Still wearing his black jacket, but with the top three studs of his shirt undone and his tie hanging loose around his neck, he looked approachably mussed and decidedly male. Undeniably attentive.

"You're very quiet. Are you having second thoughts?"

Second, third. Carmen smiled. Up here, alone with him, away from the rest of the world, anything seemed possible. Up here, alone with him, everything seemed right.

She sipped her wine, looking back into the night and the city thirty stories below. It was what happened down there that had her running scared.

"I wanted you to enjoy yourself tonight."

She knew he was watching her. "I did. Very much."

"But . . ." he prompted. When she didn't respond, he pressed her. "I hear a qualifier in there, Carmen. But what? Tell me what went wrong."

Where did she start? With the elite restaurant he'd taken her to, where she'd felt as out of place as a water spot on Waterford crystal? With the business associates who had stopped by their table, politely satisfying their curiosity while carefully concealing their surprise at seeing him with a woman who was outside their circle? With one particularly stunning woman who had blatantly followed her to the ladies' room and with veiled comments and not-so-veiled innuendos, let her know she was outclassed and outgunned?

"Carmen . . ."

She closed her eyes and shook her head.

"Carmen, what did Victoria say to you tonight?"

"Nothing. Nothing I didn't already know." Very slowly she turned her head and looked at him. "She simply pointed out the fact that I don't belong with you. That I don't belong here. And she was right. You're only deluding yourself if you think that I do."

"What I think," he said, facing her squarely, "is that you're the one woman who can make a difference in my life. What I think," he continued, cupping her face gently in his hand, "is that nothing anyone else says matters. The only words that matter are the ones that pass between us. Say the words, Carmen," he whispered, drawing her slowly toward him, "say the words I want to hear."

NINE

Her eyes glittered, their darkness and vast beauty rivaled only by the star-studded sky. In their shimmering depths Logan saw the reflection of his own fierce longing. In the part of him that housed his awakening heart, he felt a love he'd never thought he'd harbor.

He knew he'd taken a risk tonight, exposing her to Houston's elite. But it was a risk that had to be taken if she were to become a part of his life.

She'd handled the assessing glances and veiled surprise as he'd known she would: With dignity and pride and a regal presence she wasn't aware she commanded. It was only now, when the ordeal was behind her, that she was letting the doubts creep back in.

He knew how to assuage them. Fair play or foul, he had every intention of doing so.

Lowering his head to hers, he touched his lips to the curve of her jaw. She shivered sweetly, whether in surrender or resistance, he neither knew nor cared. Tomorrow was soon enough to deal with her doubts. Tonight he was going to show her what really mattered.

"Say the words, Carmen," he whispered again, spreading his fingers wide along her throat and sipping his way to her mouth.

He tipped her head back to give himself better access to the soft underside of her jaw and breathed in her intoxicating fragrance. Her lashes brushed like Spanish lace against her cheeks as he touched his mouth to the corner of hers, seeking admittance.

When her lips parted, he drew her lower lip between his teeth. He nipped her lightly, then soothed her tender flesh with the slow stroke of his tongue.

"Say the words."

An intimate brush of his hips against her belly, an erotic promise at the delicate shell of her ear, made her sigh tremulously. With a moan of surrender, she moved against him like summer mist, all quivering, giving woman.

On a low, ragged groan, he folded her into his arms for a deep, drugging kiss. She tasted of temptation and desire, excitement and passion, and a longing made fragile by her vulnerability.

With his hand still caressing her throat, he broke the kiss and searched her eyes. And in her eyes he found the answer he needed.

The words he craved suddenly ceased to matter. What she told him without them was everything he needed to know. What she showed him with her body was the only response he required.

Tucking her protectively against his side, he walked her from the balcony, through the penthouse, to his bedroom. When they stopped beside his bed, his hoarse whisper sounded strained, even to his own ears. "I've wanted you since the first time I saw you."

"Yes." A breathless confirmation. A guileless affirmation.

The delicate beat of her pulse fluttered fast and wild along the slender column of her throat. He leaned to press a kiss there, a kiss that turned into a lengthy caress of lips and teeth and tongue. He felt a shiver that answered his own run though her. Felt the weakness of his own control as well.

"I thought you were an angel," he admitted as he framed her face in his hands, then threaded his fingers through the heavy satin of her hair. "The first time I saw you . . . I thought I was dreaming. Sometimes . . ." He stopped and swallowed hard as he lowered his hands to the jeweled buckle of her belt. "Sometimes I still wonder if I am."

He was aware that his hands were shaking as the buckle gave way and he let the belt drop to the floor. His heart double-pumped when her dress fell open to reveal the satin and lace of her black lingerie, the caramel and cream of her skin.

Jealous of the night shadows that caressed her, he leaned to turn on the bedside lamp. "Angel," he whispered, watching her face in the pale lamplight.

He brushed the silk from her shoulders. It pooled in a vivid red puddle at her feet. "Do you have any idea how badly I want to see you in my bed?"

With a slow flutter of her lashes, with a breath-stealing drop of her eyes, she satisfied that want. A shy angel, a sultry seductress, she slipped out of her high-heel shoes, then reclined on her back in the middle of his bed.

Her long, slim legs were covered to midthigh by sheer black stockings. The lace straps of her garter belt arrowed provocatively toward the wispy scrap of bikini panties that matched her smoky-black bra.

Satin and seduction, innocence and acquiescence, her dark eyes never left his as she fanned her hair like a wild mane about her head and lay there, open and vulnerable to him. A gesture of trust. A declaration of need.

He shrugged out of his jacket, ripped off his shirt, and made quick work of his shoes and socks.

"You are so very beautiful." His weight sank into the bed beside her. Twisting at the hip, he braced his hands at either side of her waist. He couldn't stop looking at her, at the picture she made lying there, the luxuriant flare of her hips, the concave of her slender waist, the generous swell of her breasts straining against the lace of her bra.

"You're everything I remembered," he whispered as he bent his head to her breast and softly nuzzled. "You feel so good. Your softness. Your taste. Being with you like this—it's all I've thought of." Opening his mouth wide, he sucked her through the lace cup of her bra.

"Have you thought of it too?" Leaving one breast for the promise of the other, equally sweet, equally responsive, he drew her deeply into his mouth. "Have you thought of this, Carmen? Of me touching you this way? Of me kissing you here . . . and here?"

"Yes." Yearning, she shivered and arched and pressed herself into his caress.

With a low, shuddering growl, he tugged the lace aside with his teeth until her breast sprang free. Playfulness gave way then to possession. Desire gave way to greed. He took her fully in his mouth, sucking and savoring and satisfying a need that had been denied too long.

He pulled away to unfasten the front clasp of her bra and peel the delicate lace aside. He watched a darkening storm build in her eyes as he cupped her breast in his palm then rubbed the tip with his thumb.

"Beautiful," he whispered as her nipple, shiny and wet from his loving, crowned in the center of a coffee-dark aureole. "Beautiful," he repeated, molding her fullness in his hand and lowering his mouth again.

Midnight dreams paled in the light of her reality. Memory faded in the wealth of the here and now. He would have drowned gladly in the taste of her and died a happy man . . . until she moved sinuously against him and, with a boldness born of her rising desire, reached for the buckle of his belt.

Her gently aggressive touch told of her urgency

and sparked his need to see her response to the effect she had on him.

Straddling her hips with his thighs, he rose to his knees above her. In silence, in communion, he relayed his wishes, then watched her face as comprehension dawned.

With trembling fingers, she undid his belt, slowly lowered his fly, and freed him.

In her eyes, he saw that she understood the power and the control she had over him.

She could bring him to his knees.

She could leave him shaken and weak.

She could make him whole and strong, empower him with her longing.

She managed to do it all when she slowly skimmed his pants and briefs down his hips, then took his tumescent length in her hands.

Her touch was delicate. Yet her caress was as bold as the uninhibited desire glittering in her eyes. And her desire drove him over the edge. Lust, love, liberation became synonymous with her name. Ultimate possession became as crucial as breathing. He rolled away from her long enough to strip off his pants, find the foil-wrapped package of protection in his bedside table, and roll it on.

When he turned back to her, she opened her arms in a silent plea of invitation.

He'd wanted this to be a night she'd remember. And as she lay there, open to him, wanton for him, he knew it was a night he would never forget.

He spread his fingers wide and low over her belly. Uninhibited in her passion, she covered his hand with her own. She rocked her hips against the slow, steady pressure of his palm. Her flesh was heated satin, her scent a lure as seductive as the night. But it was her trust that was his undoing, a trust she offered as freely and as implicitly as her love.

"Please," she whispered, arching into his touch as his fingers slipped beneath the triangle of black lace and delved into her liquid heat.

"Here?" he whispered, watching the desire in her eyes fire to smoky passion as he stroked her. "Like this?"

"Yes . . ." A soft, tremulous shudder.

"And this . . ."

"Yessss . . ." A wild, reckless cry.

Pushing her panties down her hips and over her legs, he covered her body with his, needing to feel her softness beneath him, aching to have her heat enfold him.

She reached for him. Winding her arms around his neck, she captured his mouth with hers and drew him down, down into her fire, down into a desire that spiraled around them as dark as midnight, as volatile as thunder.

She arched her hips against him in blatant invitation and unmistakable promise. Driven by her restlessness, he parted her thighs with his knee and, on a long, deep stroke, penetrated the sweet haven she offered. She was hot and tight, so hot he felt the burn, so tight he was afraid he'd hurt her. Yet when she rose to meet him, wet and welcome with wanting, he had to force himself to slow down.

With a ragged moan, he pulled out. Bracing himself above her, he fought for control.

"Come back."

Shaken by the depth of his need, possessed by her answering passion, he almost lost it then. He entered her again, slowly this time, inch by exquisite inch, until he was once more buried deep inside the part of her he swore no other man would ever know.

When her body clenched around him like a tight, velvet fist, he groaned and withdrew.

"Again," she whispered, reaching for his hips to guide him back to her.

Sweat beaded across the taut muscles of his back as he poised above her, holding back, holding strong, waiting to hear the words that were suddenly as important to him as the moment.

"Please," she pleaded, moving into him. Restless, needy, she locked her ankles around his hips and urged him back inside her.

"Please what, Carmen? Tell me what you want."

He watched her face, witnessed her need as she reached between their bodies and touched him, caressing him until he thought his resolve would shatter.

"I want you. Inside me."

"I want you, *Logan*," he gritted out between

clenched teeth. Suddenly he needed to hear the word he had tried to convince himself held little importance. A word he'd never heard her say. One word that made all the difference. "Say it, Carmen. Say my name."

Her eyes, aflame with passion, went soft and misty with understanding.

Touching a hand to his hair, she guided his mouth to hers for a deep, desperate kiss. "I want you, Logan," she murmured, her sweet breath mingling with his. "Only you, Logan . . . always and only you," she promised on a reedy whisper, and with the pressure of her heels at the small of his back, invited him to come back home.

With her words and her sighs to guide him, he filled her again, slowly at first. Then, driven wild by her breathy little gasps of building passion, he drove into her with fast, deep strokes. He was consumed by the thought of making her his. To physically possess her until he erased any doubt about his love for her from her mind. To relentlessly claim her until she understood she belonged to him.

He wanted her thinking only of him. He wanted her aware only of him, of his love for her, of his desire for her, of the absolute beauty of their lovemaking and the strength of the two of them together.

She cried his name and with heightening urgency matched the action of his hips. Her breath fluttered against his shoulder, hot and ragged as she clutched him tighter, begging for release, pleading for forever, chanting his name like a hushed, reverent prayer.

When he felt the first convulsive little tremor ripple through her body, he, too, surrendered. On a long, shuddering breath, he plunged deep. His release was so explosive he felt suspended somewhere between a sweet, shattering death and a divine, sated delirium.

In the dark of night, in the silence separating their lovemaking, Logan held her close to his side.

Now that he knew what it felt like to experience her love and her passion, he didn't want to give her an opportunity to feel insecure.

"Stay with me," he whispered. "Stay the night."

She was very quiet before stirring gently against him. He felt her denial even before she began to voice it. "I don't think—"

Rising to an elbow, he silenced her with a long, tender kiss. "Don't think. Not tonight, Carmen. Just feel."

He lowered his mouth to the gentle curve of her shoulder and kissed her there. Nuzzling his way lazily to the delicate protrusion of her collarbone, he sipped and licked his way to the center of her breast. Laving her nipple with his tongue, he alternately nipped and kissed and sucked until he felt her shiver and moan and finally melt beneath the persuasion of his mouth.

"Feel good?" he whispered against the flesh he'd wet with his tongue, delighting at the chill bumps of response that rose on her skin.

"Yes."

She looked both pagan and pure as she stretched like a sleek, tempting tigress.

"And this?" he asked, dipping his tongue into the sweet indentation of her naval.

When she moaned in answer, he moved lower, tasting the soft, giving flesh of her belly. He kissed the inside of one soft, supple thigh, then the other before moving to the part of her he had yet to taste.

She raised up on her elbows, her eyes wide with question, with guarded alarm, and with a very new and forbidden excitement.

"Logan—"

"Shhh . . ." Watching the shock in her eyes turn to a trembling anticipation, then a dark, exotic pleasure, he pressed his mouth to the black curls sheltering her femininity.

At the first intimate stroke of his tongue, her head fell back. At the next, deeper stroke, she collapsed onto his pillow with a moan, her hands clutching convulsively at the sheets beneath her.

Cradling her hips in his hands, he lifted her to his mouth, wanting to take her higher, wanting to savor and seduce and love her until his was the only name she would remember.

She tasted of sex and secrets, of woman and desire. His woman, his desire. Her love was selfless with wonder, innocent and new.

Only when she cried out and came apart for him,

only when she lay limp and languid and gloriously wasted, did he ease back up her body.

He gathered her tightly in his arms while she trembled. "Still want to go home?" he whispered against her temple.

A small, sated chuckle rippled through her limp body. With supreme effort, she raised a hand to caress his jaw. "I couldn't go anywhere, and you know it."

"And that, sweet Carmen," he said, smiling against her hair, "was the general idea."

He was sleeping. In the middle of his bed, in the middle of the night, Carmen huddled against the headboard, hugging a pillow to her chest. His shirt was draped over her shoulders. For long, intimate moments she watched him sleep.

He was sprawled on his stomach, gloriously sated, the sheet falling low over his hips. Her heart fluttered at the thought of the masculinity it covered. He was a beautiful man. He was a beautiful lover.

And she was a woman in love.

Without stopping to think, she touched his hair. He stirred and reached for her. When he didn't find her where he wanted her, he rose on his elbows and looked around until he saw her shadowed against the headboard.

"I'm sorry I woke you."

Rolling over on his side, he wiped the sleep from his eyes with a rough sweep of his broad hand, then reached for her again. Without a word, he pulled her back beneath him and slipped inside her with an ease and an urgency that left her breathless.

"Still sorry?" he asked against her breast as he arched his back and took her into his mouth.

"Only . . ." She gasped as he rolled them together until he was spread-eagle on his back and she was brazenly astride him. "Only that I waited so long."

He chuckled, a rich, glorious rumble of a supremely confident male. "Then by all means," he murmured, settling her deeper over his heat, "let's make up for lost time."

His strong hands spanned her waist as he urged her into a rhythm as timeless as the love she felt for him and as lush as the act they were sharing.

"You must think I'm shameless," she whispered when they'd both recovered and were drifting sleepily in the aftermath.

He hugged her hard. "Shameless. Wanton. A natural-born brazen hussy."

He grunted when her elbow found its mark and dug into his ribs.

"And sexy and soft," he added, his teasing grin fading, "Carmen, you're the softest woman I've ever known."

"And you've known a lot of women."

She hated herself in that moment. She hated the jealousy she had no right to feel, she hated the slight tremor in her voice that conveyed her insecurity.

"I told you I'd never lie to you again," he said

softly. "I'm not going to go back on that promise. Yes, there've been women. But never a woman who meant to me what you do. Never a woman who made a tinker's damn worth of difference in my life before I met you."

She wanted to believe him. Lying in his arms as he held her, idly stroking her hair, his strong, sleek body a haven to shelter her doubts, she found it easy to envision the two of them together forever. But here, in his bed, was the illusion. Here, in his arms, was the fantasy.

"Spend the day with me."

His hand stilled in her hair when he felt the sudden tension in her body.

"I . . . I don't have any clothes."

If her panicky grasp at that ridiculous straw of escape bothered him, he didn't show it. He simply rose up and grinned rakishly down at her. "I don't anticipate that you'll be needing any."

Giving up and giving in to the moment and the man and the magic he made her feel, she let go of her doubt. She smiled up at him. "Has anyone ever accused you of being manipulative?"

"Never to my face, angel. And you're the only one I'd ever let get by with it."

"Yeah?"

"Yeah."

Emboldened by his admission, excited by the invitation in his eyes, she decided to test his indulgence even further.

"And what else might you be of a mind to let me get by with?"

His grin was nothing short of lethal as he lay back on the bed, his arms spread wide in a demonstration of his willingness to subject himself to her brand of manipulation.

"Why don't you put it to the test and see?"

He passed the test with flying colors.

When he roused her later to feed her breakfast, an inherent shyness caused her to insist that regardless of his ease with his nakedness, she needed something to wear.

She slipped into his champagne-colored dress shirt. The exquisite, tailor-made shirt of watery silk felt like a cloud caressing her body and made the dress she'd been so proud to wear for him the night before seem like burlap in comparison. The fact that one button on the cuff of this shirt probably cost more than her dress suddenly diminished the pleasure she'd felt being squired around on his arm.

It was only one of the myriad contrasts between his world and hers, and stirred her doubts to life again. She sat at his elegant dining-room table, shoving the omelet he'd made her around her plate with a fork. A gold-plated fork. An outrageously ornate and fragile plate.

"Much as the idea appeals to me, Carmen," he said, looking thoughtful as he rested his forearms on the table, "I can't keep you in bed forever. But if you're going to get that look on your face every time you stop and look around you, I'm going to have to give it a try."

She glanced at him, then away.

"Carmen, these"—he made an expansive gesture that took in the opulent furnishings of the penthouse— "these are only things. They're no threat to you. And they have no meaning for me. You. You are the only thing here that matters."

She folded her hands in her lap and leaned back to look at him. "I don't think you're being realistic about this," she said in a small but determined voice.

He scowled. "Realistic?"

"There are things about me that you don't know."

"The same could be said of me."

"*Nothing* about us is the same Logan," she insisted, willing him to see things from her perspective.

"If you're talking about wealth, if you're talking about background . . . if you're talking, as I suspect, about heritage . . . Carmen, surely you realize by now none of it makes any difference."

"It makes all the difference."

"To you?"

"To how you'll come to perceive me. To how you'll eventually react when the people who are close to you make it clear that who I am, what I am, makes a difference to them."

"Why don't you let me worry about them? Why don't you give me a chance to prove how little it matters? Carmen, the only thing that matters is that I love you."

Her eyes widened.

"It surprises you so much?" He smiled gently. "Truth to tell, it surprised me too. But there it is, isn't it? I don't want to deny it any longer. And I don't want you to doubt it."

Panic, pure and piercing, provoked an almost uncontrollable urge to run.

"Don't shut me out, Carmen." Rising in all his naked glory, he came to her. "Don't blame the sins of ignorance and the prejudice of generations on me."

He knelt beside her and took her hand in his. "I'm one man. I'm the one man who loves you because of who you are, not because of who you think I need you to be. And because you are the one woman who has made me aware how special life can be with someone like you to share it."

She wanted so badly to believe that all that mattered was the love she felt for him and the trust he offered as a condition of his love.

But would he think she was so special if he knew where she'd come from? Absolute poverty is not pretty. Absolute poverty is often ugly and dark. She'd never known her father. He'd taken off long before she was born. She'd never known her mother. She'd known an addict who, devastated by the course her life had taken, had OD'd when Carmen was just thirteen. The only thing coming between her and the same path her mother had taken was a special lady who encouraged her to finish school and work her way through nurses' training. She'd been one of the lucky ones. And though her existence was Spartan compared to his, it was grandiose compared with what she'd come from.

"Carmen, it doesn't have to be so scary. Where we came from isn't as meaningful as what we do. We work, we try to make a difference. But because of what you perceive as a problem, if you don't give this a chance, we'll both end up with less than we deserve. We'll both end up alone—thinking of each other, wishing we were together. Is it so wrong, what we want?" he continued, earnestly searching her face. "Does it have to be so complicated?"

"Yes," she whispered, clinging to her resolve to maintain some perspective.

He touched her then. And that soft brush of his hand on her thigh turned her yes into a no.

When he touched her, nothing was complicated. Everything was simple. As simple as the slow, languorous glide of his fingers across her skin, stroking, seeking, finding that part of her that responded with shameless desire. As simple as the immediate, responsive need he evoked with his touch.

She gasped as he tugged her effortlessly to the floor, flicked open the buttons of the shirt she wore, and laid it open.

"I don't believe in complications," he whispered. He rose and lifted her, then gently deposited her on the carpet. He covered her body with his and swiftly entered her. "When you're beneath me, when I'm inside you, nothing is complicated. Everything is simple, and settled and right."

She closed her eyes and held him there, letting the strength of his body surround her, letting the cadence of his hips seduce her into believing what he insisted was true.

Could it be this simple? Could it be as easy as the swift, explosive awakening he kindled inside her with a look, a touch.

Her heart thundered as he braced himself on his hands and looked down into her eyes.

"I'm not giving up on this," he promised, his eyes dark and determined, his voice husky with his own attempt to control his desire. "I'm not giving in. I want you in my life, and later, when you're trying to convince yourself you don't belong in mine, I want you to remember how it feels when I'm inside you."

He moved slowly, sinuously, driving her wild, nurturing her need until she was clinging, and trembling and urging him deeper.

"I want you to remember," he commanded, lowering his mouth to hers and teasing her with the whisper of his breath against her skin, the glide of his tongue across her parted lips. "Remember every time we've come together. Remember the heat, the hunger"—he thrust deep—" . . . and the love, Carmen. Remember . . ." He groaned and stroked them both to a stunning, explosive conclusion. "Remember most of all the love."

His whispered request filtered through the haze, riding the currents of the whirlwind that slowly drifted out of their path . . . gone but, as he intended, never forgotten.

TEN

Though Logan had been born to wealth, he hadn't amassed greater riches by relying on what he insisted was an accident of birth. He worked hard. In business and in love, Carmen was soon to learn. He was tenacious, driven, determined. And he was as devoted to making her see the possibility of sharing their lives as she was to making him see the impossibility.

A consummate businessman, he wasn't above taking every advantage to arrive at the end he desired. Nothing was off limits—including Juan.

Because of Logan's influence, gaining access to Juan, always a frustration to Carmen before, suddenly ceased to be a problem. While it irritated her that his money and power could accomplish what she couldn't, she embraced every opportunity to see Juan. She cherished the man and the boy as the gifts that they were.

With Logan making the requests, day trips, afternoon visits, even an extra overnighter became the norm, not the exception. Logan appeared committed to sharing both her life and Juan's—and this included demonstrating to her the advantages sharing with him could bring.

During the next few weeks the three of them laughed and played and learned about love and patience and understanding. She became aware of a change in both Logan and Juan that was touching, heartwarming. Juan, under Logan's careful attention, gained more and more confidence in himself. And Logan seemed to her to come to terms with the child inside himself that she suspected he'd never been given the opportunity to know.

She came to terms with a few things too. When Juan couldn't be a part of their times together, Logan had a willing student in Carmen, and he taught her about the power of emotional love as a complement to their physical relationship. The love he made was exquisite. The pleasures he gave, selfless.

Little by little he was making her a believer. Little by little she was beginning to accept the possibility that he really loved her. That a future for them together might actually be something worth contemplating. Exactly what part he intended for her to play in that future was still uncertain.

He talked of want, of need, even of love, but never of marriage. She was glad he shied away from mentioning it.

And then, too, looming over it all, was the unanswered question of whether Juan would play a part in any future they might have. The court date drew nearer. The prospect of the judge ruling in favor of returning Juan to his mother, who had completed extensive court-ordered sessions to learn parenting skills, hung like an ominous cloud above them.

"Why the sad face?" Logan asked as he drove Carmen home from a quiet, candlelit dinner at his penthouse. It had been a dinner spiced with long sultry looks that had culminated in an exquisitely sensual session in his arms and his bed.

"Sorry." She forced a smile, not wanting to cast a shadow over the wonderful evening they'd shared. "I guess I'm sad the night has to end."

Juan's future constantly rode on the edge of her thoughts. She didn't want Logan to know the extent of her concern. He'd already done so much to make sure they had time together.

"It didn't have to end," he reminded her softly. "You could have spent the night."

"Not and work tomorrow, I couldn't." Her voice dropped to a low intimate murmur. "I don't seem to manage to get much sleep in your bed."

A knowing smile passed between them as he pulled up in front of her apartment. Their smiles combined longing and hunger and the wonder of the love they made every time they came together. The pleasures they shared were a phenomenon that bred a heady, breathless anticipation for the next time . . . and the next.

"For the record," he said, drawing her against him and touching his lips to her hair as they walked to her door, "if you didn't have to work tomorrow and if I didn't have to fly to New Orleans in the morning, I'd have found a way to keep you there."

Somewhere between the drive and the determination to call it an early night, she'd begun to miss him, even though he hadn't gone yet.

"You're too used to getting your own way, Mr. Prince," she replied primly. Leaning back against the door, she tempted him with a deliberately come-hither smile. "It doesn't always have to be *your* bed, you know."

Bracing a palm on the door beside her head, he grinned down at her. "I thought you had concerns about an early morning."

"I do. That's why I need a good night's sleep." She lowered her lashes and added in a voice full of innuendo and promise, "Something tells me if you come in for a little while, I'll sleep like a baby."

His sexy grin deepened along with the color of his eyes. "You had in mind that I tuck you in?"

His husky suggestion sent a shiver eddying through her body. She wrapped her fingers around his tie and tugged him closer. "Something like that."

"Lord, I'm going to miss you," he whispered against her mouth as he folded her tightly against him.

"Miss me tomorrow." She nipped him lightly, her insides turning liquid at the exquisite crush of his body against hers. "Make love to me again."

On a deep, throaty groan, he drew her into a kiss that sparked a flame to life between them. Fumbling fingers and questing hands worked frantically at knots and buttons and, belatedly, at the key to her door.

With her giggling and him growling and both of them lost in an insatiable need to claim each other, they tumbled inside her apartment, where Logan promptly stripped her blouse from one shoulder and pinned her hard against the door.

She was working hurriedly at the buckle of his belt when a sudden feeling set all her senses humming. Abruptly stilling her hands, she looked over Logan's shoulder and froze. The silhouette of a man whose features were hidden in the shadows of the dark apartment moved slowly toward them.

She stiffened and whispered Logan's name. Even in the heat of his passion he recognized the stark terror in her abruptly rigid stance and in the breathless quality of her voice.

He pulled away and saw that her wide-eyed gaze was locked unflinchingly on something beyond his shoulder. He spun around, effectively shielding her with his body.

"Take it easy, man," Logan said calmly, pulling Carmen more securely behind him as he sized up the dark figure watching them. "Whatever you want—it's yours. Just take it and go. No one needs to get hurt."

In silence, in anticipation, the man moved to the lamp by the sofa and flicked it on.

"Rico," Carmen cried when the light revealed his features. She slumped against the door in relief as the adrenaline flow slowed to a rate that made both breathing and talking possible. "My God, you scared me to death."

She straightened, intending to go to him, a slow smile forming. Logan's hand on her arm stopped her. It was only then that she became aware of the lingering tension in Logan's body and of the antagonistic looks passing between him and her brother.

Animosity hummed like the threat of an explosion.

"Rico," she said, attempting to defuse the tension. "I didn't know you were coming home."

"Obviously." Rico's dark gaze swung from Logan's to hers. Instead of warming as she'd expected when he looked at her, his anger intensified with accusation. "Just like I didn't want to believe Dallas when he told me what might be going on here."

"You saw Johnny?"

Rico's gaze darted from her to Logan. "He called me. And he filled me in on the sweet deal your 'friend' here made with him. It seems he's been busy making more deals with you." His fists and his jaw worked in tandem. "I never thought I'd see the day when my sister would become a rich Anglo's whore."

If he had struck her, he couldn't have staggered her more. Reeling with the pain of his insult, she could only stare. Logan suffered no such problem.

"You little punk," Logan said, striding toward Rico with blood lust in his eyes.

"Logan, no," she cried, shocked into action by the rage in his voice. "He didn't mean that. He doesn't understand."

"I understand, all right," Rico said acidly, his gaze sweeping in disgust over Carmen's disheveled blouse and tangled hair. "And you're only fooling yourself if you think you mean anything more to him than a piece of Spanish—"

Logan's fist cracked into Rico's mouth before he could finish his crude and hurtful slur.

Rico's head snapped to the side as he fell back onto the sofa. Logan followed him down with all the rage of a bull scenting blood.

"Logan. No!" Carmen screamed. Pleading with him to stop, she squeezed between Logan's upraised fist and her brother. "Please," she begged, when he froze to avoid hitting her. "Please. Don't do this. Let me talk to him. I'll make him understand."

Very slowly, his gaze never leaving Rico's, Logan backed away. Squaring his shoulders, he watched Rico with a barely controlled outrage. "You owe your sister an apology."

Rico rose, wiping blood from his mouth. "I owe her nothing. And I owe you even less. Get out of my home. Now. And I don't ever want you coming near my sister again."

Heartsick, Carmen ran a hand through her hair and stepped between them again. "Stop it! Both of you. This is ridiculous."

"One of us goes, Carmen," Rico threatened with

none of the rancor leaving his voice. "Remember your place . . . and remember your people before you decide which one walks out the door."

"Look," she began, weary suddenly of this entire scene. "If you'll cool that hot head of yours for a few minutes—"

Drilling her with a look of anger and disgust, Rico grabbed his duffel bag and headed for the door. She cast Logan a pleading look.

Swearing under his breath, he moved in front of the door, blocking Rico's exit.

"I need to talk to him." She met his eyes beseechingly. "Please, Logan. It would be best if you left us alone. I'm sorry," she added when his eyes narrowed. "Try to understand."

She could see that he was trying, but it was a deep reach and one he didn't willingly make. Finally he capitulated. A major concession for a man used to getting his own way.

"I'll call you in the morning," he said after a long, tense moment. He shot Rico a glare that should have made him shudder. "Lay one hand on her and you'll answer to me."

Rico's answering frown was both insolent and rebellious. "You would do well to remember your place here, too, Anglo. You don't own me. And you may have paid for her, but you don't own my sister either. Not anymore."

Carmen gasped, more angry now than hurt by her brother's cutting accusations. "Logan. I'm sorry.

But please, please go now. We'll talk in the morning."

Planted like a tree in the doorway, Logan looked ready to explode again.

"He won't hurt me, for heaven's sake," she insisted, hating to push him out the door, but knowing she'd never get this resolved with the testosterone levels so high in both men. "It's okay. Please, please go."

With a last, lingering look at Carmen, a last explicit but silent threat to Rico, he turned and stalked out.

Closing the door behind him, Carmen sagged against it and breathed a sigh of relief. The relief, however, was short-lived when she saw the anger in her brother's eyes.

"Dammit, Rico." She headed for the bathroom and her first-aid supplies. "And damn men in general. Why is it always *my* apartment that turns into a war zone?" She returned quickly to treat her brother's battered mouth.

He pulled away as if he couldn't bear to have her touch him. "Why, Carmen? Why did you let a man like that use you?"

She sighed deeply. It was going to be a long night.

It was even longer than she'd anticipated. When the smoke cleared and neither had given any ground, she threw up her hands and went to bed—where Rico's accusations kept her awake well into the night.

He was wrong about Logan using her. He was wrong. In her heart, she knew that. But he was right about everything else. She had let her love for Logan blind her to the differences between them. His people would never accept her. Her people would never accept him.

She'd lost sight of those simple truths. She *had* forgotten where she'd come from. She had forgotten where *he* had come from.

Getting through the next day was pure torture. And as if Rico's sullen contempt and her own resurrected doubts weren't enough misery to contend with, there was the unexpected visitor who arrived shortly after she returned home from work the next afternoon.

Even without his cool, polite introduction, she would have recognized Logan's father anywhere. Preston Prince's genes were strong. As she stared at him she knew she was seeing Logan thirty years in the future.

"You're very lovely, my dear," an older, harder, but no less devastatingly attractive Prince observed when Carmen opened her door for him. "I can see why my son is so taken with you."

While his words were eloquent and flattering, the tone of his voice was redolent with contempt. "But let's cut to the chase, shall we?" he suggested as he stepped into the apartment and gave a cursory and condescending look around him. "How much?"

Though she returned the diamond-hard stare of

blue eyes a colder shade of Logan's, it was a moment before she found her voice.

"I beg your pardon?"

He smiled. Glacially cool. Regally authoritative. "How much, my dear? How much will it take to get you out of his life permanently."

She regarded him with a frosty contempt of her own. "That's the second time in the past twelve hours that someone has accused me of being for sale. One accusation I can excuse due to immaturity. Yours, there is no excuse for."

Her pride surprised him. He looked at her again—with no more respect, but at least with a grudging admiration.

"You're very good," he said thoughtfully. "Perhaps I've underestimated you. All right, let's explore this thoroughly, then. The way I see it, you've already been compensated to some degree, so it's only a question of arriving at your final price."

"Compensated?" she said, confused, yet mesmerized by his coldness and his unmitigated gall.

"The boy," he said impatiently. "Surely you know how much it cost Logan to ensure custody went to you."

Her heart jumped to her throat. "What are you talking about?"

"Now that's intriguing," he said, eyeing her with renewed interest when he recognized that her shock was real. "Logan hasn't told you, has he?"

"Told me what?"

"He's yours, Ms. Sanchez. The little deaf child. Logan arranged it."

A growing unease outdistanced her outrage. "The hearing isn't until next week."

"The hearing will be canceled when the judge is advised that the mother no longer wishes to maintain custody of her son and that her wish is for custody to be granted to you." He smiled again. Again without warmth. Again without compassion. "Money does have its advantages—but then, you've already recognized that fact, haven't you?"

She felt suddenly cold inside. Cold and at the same time elated that Juan's future with her was secure. But at what cost? To know that he'd been bought and paid for like a piece of furniture or a shiny new toy—could she live with that kind of guilt? Could she live with herself knowing that money paid on her behalf took advantage of Juan's mother's ignorance and poverty?

Numb, she closed her eyes and turned away from the man she was having increasing difficulty believing was Logan's father. He was heartless. Calculating. As much as she felt pity for Juan's mother, in this moment she felt even more pity for Logan. And more disgust for his father.

"Please leave, Mr. Prince," she said in the suddenly quiet room.

His footsteps fell heavily, then stopped behind her. He slid a sealed envelope onto the top of an end table.

"You're an intelligent woman. I'm hoping threats

won't be necessary." He paused when she turned to face him, angry at herself for allowing a degree of fear to rattle her.

"There's a good deal of cash inside that envelope, Ms. Sanchez," he continued as if he'd never uttered the word *threat*. "Enough for you and the boy to live on comfortably. Enough for you to relocate to a place where all this can be left behind you. To a place where Logan won't be reminded of this"—he paused as if searching for the right word—"infatuation he feels for you."

She faced him grimly, ice in her voice and her eyes. "Logan is a man, Mr. Prince. Infatuation seems a bit inappropriate, wouldn't you say?"

"I was trying to be kind, my dear," he said, no trace of kindness in his voice or in his expression. "But if you insist, let me rephrase. When Logan comes to his senses and realizes it's not love but lust drawing him to you, you'll be far enough away that he'll be able to seek his diversions elsewhere."

She shivered, despite the heated anger pulsing through her. "You are disgusting."

Unflinching, he leveled her with a look both superior and intimidating. "Take the money, Ms. Sanchez. Take the money and leave. If you don't, I'll see to it that you never see the boy again. And I'll guarantee you that Logan will know every detail of your past, from your illegitimacy to your mother's unfortunate addiction."

She took a step back, the ruthless intent in his eyes frightening her.

"Oh, and just so there's no confusion on this issue, my son is never to know of this visit or the deal is off. Surely you can see the monetary advantages of keeping your silence. And given your special charms"—his gaze raked over her insultingly—"I'm sure you'll be able to convince him that the decision to break it off was entirely yours."

His eyes were hard and piercing. Without another word, he turned and walked out the door.

Carmen sat on the sill of her open bedroom window, breathing in the scent and the sounds of the rare and welcome rain from the storm. The heat of the streets and the dust in the air mingled with the downpour. A faint and oddly cleansing breeze gently stirred the curtains at her open window and cooled her skin.

Midnight was a time for reflection for her. For Rico, it was a time to prowl. She smiled when she thought of her hotheaded brother. She loved him fiercely. He loved her, too, even though he couldn't see past his anger at the moment. She knew that in time it would pass. And she smiled to herself, feeling a distant sympathy for some unknown and unfortunate woman whose heart Rico would toy with tonight in an attempt to forget his anger.

She heard the soft click of a key in her lock—a sound she'd been expecting. A man she'd been expecting. And an end she was determined to live with.

❧————————————❧

Logan's steps never faltered as he walked directly to Carmen's bedroom. He stopped in the doorway when he saw her silhouetted against the window frame.

"It's beautiful, isn't it?" she said softly, her head turned toward the rain and the night.

The light from the neon sign flashed familiarly and threw a rainbow of colors over her lustrous hair. She was beautiful. As vibrant as the night. As luminous as the sky lit by streaks of lightning. And as unsettled and as volatile as the storm.

As much as he wanted to go to her and take her in his arms, something kept him from it. Something in her voice. Something in the tense set of her shoulders. Something in his gut that warned him away.

"Beautiful? I guess that depends on your perspective," he said cautiously. "Now that I'm on the ground, I can feel a bit more benevolent toward the wind and the lightning."

She turned to face him then. "Odd you should use that word. I was thinking in terms of your father's benevolence."

Ignoring the dampness seeping through his jacket, he walked slowly toward her. "My father?"

Her dark eyes searched his face in the storm glow. A stark, black stillness came over him. Numb with foreboding, he forced himself to ask, "What does my father have to do with anything?"

Her eyes were glistening as she looked at him in that moment before she slowly rose. Without a word, she walked to the small table by her bed, removed an envelope from the top drawer, and handed it to him.

He stared at the envelope, opened it, and thumbed through the cash inside.

"You should be pleased." Her voice, like her gaze, was as cool as the wind, as distant as the rumbling thunder. "He places a high value on preserving your freedom."

He closed his eyes, battling a rage unlike anything he'd ever known. "The bastard."

"You judge him, yet you employ his methods."

He snapped his gaze to hers.

"Juan," she said simply, answering the question in his eyes.

"You know about that. How?"

"Does it matter?"

He watched her carefully. Accusation, anger, and disappointment showed on her face.

"What matters," he said, countering her anger, "is your happiness. And Juan's."

"At his mother's expense?" Her voice was quietly cutting.

"At his mother's request," he replied finally.

"But that's implying she had a choice."

"Carmen," he said, easing a hip onto the windowsill opposite her and facing her squarely. "I thought I'd made an arrangement that would be beneficial to everyone."

She shook her head sadly. "How can you talk so calmly about arranging people's lives? You took her son away from her. You bought and paid for him, the same way you bought and paid for Johnny's cooperation. How does that make you better than your father, who thinks he can buy and pay for me?"

He searched her eyes and found nothing but anger there. Anger and disgust and a coldly distant judgment he was suddenly very weary of fighting.

"Well," he said, feeling himself withdraw his emotions behind the wall he'd erected long before he'd met her. "It would appear that my father, at least, was on target. In the end, it came down to what it always comes down to. Money. Obviously you had no qualms about keeping it."

But the defense wasn't working. He was still feeling. And he reacted to the pain in her eyes and to his own feeling of betrayal like an animal whose wounds were raw and bleeding. Bottom line, she'd taken the money. Bottom line, she was no different than all the others.

Reaching for her, he drew her forcefully into his arms, wanting to lash out and hurt her in return. "Since your price was so high, let's see you deliver on what my father paid for."

Ignoring her wounded eyes, he drew her roughly into his kiss. He wanted nothing more than to hurt her the way her lack of trust and her ultimate betrayal had hurt him.

But the taste of her sweet mouth, the sound of

her desperate plea, the gentle warmth of her body struggling against him as he forced her down on her bed broke through the rage.

"Damn you," he swore, wrenching himself away from her. "Damn you," he repeated, anguished that the hate boiling up inside him ran in such close tandem to love.

Why did she have to come into his sterile, uncomplicated life and make him want to believe in something he'd known all along was a lie? And why, once he'd crossed over the line, couldn't she simply have believed in him?

She'd been right from the beginning. The differences were too vast. The obstacles were too many. Her brother, his father, a lifetime of conditioning himself not to care.

"I can't fight them all," he mumbled tiredly, then realizing he'd spoken out loud, pulled himself together.

"Enjoy the money, Carmen," he said, one last parting barb a necessity for his pride as he made his way toward the door. "You earned it—even though the price was high."

ELEVEN

"Misery loves company, you know," Barb reminded Carmen as they left Ben Taub together at the end of a double shift. "It would do you good to talk about it. And I've got to tell you, if I have to look at that long face of yours many more nights, you're going to have me crying. Big crocodile tears. We're talking flood here. Load the ark. Then my mascara will run. And you know how I hate it when that happens.

"Come on," Barb chided gently when she won the grin she'd been playing for. "Do us both a favor. I'll buy the beer."

"All right already." Agreeing reluctantly but realizing that putting up with two weeks of her moping around was above and beyond the call—even for a friend like Barb—Carmen gave in.

Two hours and a pitcher later Barb had heard enough—she'd also drunk enough, polishing off almost all the beer.

"I really can't figure you out," Barb said. "You are the most compassionate, empathetic person I know, yet you've tried this man, led him to the gallows, and all but pulled the trapdoor without ever hearing his side of the story."

Difficult as it was to admit it, Carmen knew Barb was right. And it wasn't a conclusion she'd reached in the past few hours. She'd had two weeks of solitude to face the prospect of life without Logan. Two lonely, miserable weeks to help her assess what she'd done to him. And what she'd done was unforgivable. She'd drawn conclusions on incomplete information. And she hadn't been within a stone's throw of fair.

When she'd recovered from Preston Prince's revelations, she'd paid Juan's mother a visit. Only then did she realize how right Logan had been. The girl was so young. Juan's deafness frightened her. She truly wanted what was best for her son and could not ever see herself providing it. She cared about him, but in a detached, distant way a stranger might feel about some poor unfortunate orphan. And she didn't want the responsibility of taking care of him.

Logan's only crime had been to arrange the best possible solution for everyone. Juan's mother would be provided with educational and financial opportunities to assist her in breaking out of her bonds of poverty. Juan would be raised in a loving home, the best Carmen could provide.

Carmen had repaid Logan for his compassion with accusations. She'd likened his actions to the deal Preston Prince had tried to cut with her. God forgive her, she'd compared him with his father.

But Logan wasn't anything like Preston Prince. Logan was kind and caring. A private and achingly vulnerable man. He'd exposed his inner weakness to her. He'd laid bare his soul. None of those confidences had been easy for him. For her to have let something other than his feelings and his actions sway her was unforgivable.

And even before this heart-to-heart with Barb, she knew she had to find a way to fix what she'd broken— if, in fact, it *was* fixable.

"And since when do you let other people rule your life?" Barb asked. "Pay attention," she ordered, pounding her fist on the table, drawing a measuring look from a barmaid who passed by.

Impervious to that look, more vocal even than usual from a little too much beer, Barb was just getting revved up. "First you let your brother interfere, then Logan's father. Lord, you're a dolt. Haven't you figured out yet that you two were doing fine until everybody else decided to put their fingers in the proverbial taco?"

Carmen grinned. "Barb, don't you think it's time to go home?"

"I'm not through with you yet," Barb insisted. She slumped back against the booth with a defeated snort. "Oh, what's the use. You're too damn stubborn. And too damn proud. Go home. Get out of my face. You disgust me."

"I love you, too, buddy," Carmen said.

Barb waved the words away as if they were pesky mosquitoes. "Love, shmuv. You wouldn't know love if it bit you on your better judgment. Face it, Sanchez. You blew it. And if you had any backbone at all, you'd go do something to fix it. Oh, and Carmen?"

"Yeah?"

"Help me to the bathroom, would you? I think I'm going to be sick."

PRINCE ENTERPRISES. The gold lettering on the double plate-glass doors of the corporate stronghold reeked of attitude and opulence; both attested to standards that had made the business the success it was today.

Carmen gripped the brass handle, pulled the door open, and strode through without looking back. Ignoring the raised eyebrows of the elegantly groomed guardian of the inner office, she swept her braid back over her shoulder and met the secretary's condescending glance without flinching.

"I'm here to see Logan Prince."

A slow, measured blink of an eye, a long, judgmental look later, the secretary smiled tightly. "Without an appointment, I'm afraid that won't be possible."

As she'd suspected, arranging a meeting with Logan Prince was the equivalent of requesting an audience with the pope.

"Please inform him that Carmen Sanchez is here. He'll see me."

With that, she turned, walked on legs she hoped didn't give away her lack of confidence, and deposited herself regally on the chrome-and-leather chair closest to the secretary's desk. With as much pomp as she could muster, and ignoring the fact that the secretary's hairdo in all probability cost more than her jeans and T-shirt put together, she crossed her legs, folded her hands on her lap, and stared a hole through the woman's forehead.

Recognizing that she was outstubborned, if not outclassed, the woman picked up the phone and punched out Ben Crenshaw's extension. Though she was shocked at Ben's immediate and explicit expression of relief, it didn't show on her face as she hung up the phone.

"Mr. Prince is unavailable, but Mr. Crenshaw will see you," she stated, grudgingly admiring the pretty, dark-haired woman, even a little envious of her apparent power over Logan Prince's right-hand man.

"Thank you," Carmen said as she rose, and on the same shaky legs that had brought her there, walked directly to the door.

Ben Crenshaw's name had come up frequently when she and Logan had been together. She recognized him on sight from Logan's description, and she recognized that the concern in his eyes had more to do with his friendship for Logan than with their business association.

"You wanted to see Logan," he stated flatly.

She nodded and looked around the tasteful but elaborately decorated office. "I had no idea his privacy would be so heavily guarded."

He considered her for a long moment. "It's not his privacy that concerns me," he said finally.

She recognized a gauntlet when it was thrown and knew immediately that she liked this man, if for no other reason than that he was Logan's friend and determined to protect him. "Then we both have Logan's best interests in mind," she replied honestly. "I need to see him. Can you arrange it?"

Whether he was extremely perceptive or just a hopeless romantic, when he'd taken her measure and decided she wasn't here to hurt Logan, he became her ally too.

"What's going on, Ben?"

Racing to keep pace with Logan's long, impatient strides, Ben clamped a hand on his arm to stop him. "Will you cool off, please? It's not my fault the old men decided to call an emergency board meeting. And for the last time I don't know what they want. They just insisted you show up at the boardroom at three o'clock sharp. Don't kill the messenger, man," he added when Logan's dark scowl swung to his, murder in his eyes. "I was just told to make sure you showed."

"This had damn well better be good," Logan muttered. "And where the hell are you going?"

"Hey." Ben raised his hands, palms open in supplication. "The request was for you not me. Good luck, and good-bye. I've got a hot date with a fax machine that as we speak is in the midst of a transmission."

Scowling as Ben hurried back down the hall, Logan yanked open the boardroom door and stalked inside.

He was met by silence and an empty room. No blue suits. No stern scowls from the corporate fathers. No stale cigar smoke hanging in the air.

Instead a fragrance that was lightly intoxicating, guilelessly provocative, drifted gently into his black mood. The first time he'd encountered that scent he'd known he would never forget it—or the woman who wore it.

In suspended silence, he watched as very slowly, the high-backed leather chair at the head of the boardroom table swiveled around until the occupant faced him. Carmen.

He felt a sudden tightening in his throat and fought a gut reaction to go to her. Fought, also, to deny the unwelcome acknowledgment of how badly he missed her. But the rapid beat of his heart overrode his determination to remain unaffected. The shifting of the ground beneath his feet made a lie of his carefully schooled indifference.

Seeing her again was hell, and did things to him no sane man would admit to experiencing. Anger, love, even an unconsciously nurtured hatred for her betrayal ricocheted through him.

A smart man would walk back out the door. Where Carmen Sanchez was concerned, he'd proven he wasn't a very smart man. He was about to prove it again.

He walked slowly into the room, resisting an urge to breathe life into the hope that accelerated the beat of his already hammering heart. Sinking stiffly into the chair at the opposite end of the table, he regarded her over steepled fingers.

"So," he said, breaking a silence grown brittle with tension. "What story did you tell Ben to lure him into your camp?"

Carmen felt the chill of Logan's words across twenty feet of gleaming walnut and the myriad unclaimed emotions that separated them.

In his eyes, in this boardroom calm, she could see how far he'd withdrawn from her. If he hadn't yet shut himself off completely, the door would soon be locked.

"No story," she said, determined to break through that door. "The truth. And for the record, Ben's allegiance is still with you."

His silence clearly indicated that this was her show; it was up to her to see it through.

She looked around the regally imposing boardroom. "I've pictured you in this setting. With your business face on. Calculated, controlled, reigning over your empire."

Expressionless, he shrugged. "It's where I belong. It's who I am."

"Once I would have believed that. Once, before I knew the kind of man you really are."

The face behind his steepled fingers remained impassive. "Why are you here, Carmen?"

None of this was easy for her. She'd never been a confrontational person. But she'd willingly become what she had to be it if meant getting him back.

Meeting his gaze, she took the plunge. "I was hoping I might reclaim the right to be with you."

Her heart sank as he considered her for a long, silent moment. Too late. She was too late. He'd shut himself off and wasn't about to let her back in.

She loved this man. It was her fault she'd driven him away. And it would be her fault if she didn't set things right between them.

"I'm here because I'm the woman who loves you," she said, braving his cold look with a conviction made strong by that love. "I'm here because you once said you were the man who loves me."

In the briefest of moments before he looked away, she saw a softening in his expression. Hope stirred to new life inside her—until his next words all but killed it.

"That didn't seem to be enough for you two weeks ago," he reminded her. "Why should I believe it's enough now?"

She smiled sadly. "We've come full circle, haven't we? Once it was you asking me to believe. Now I'm asking the same of you."

He was watching her carefully. Searching, she knew, for the strength it would take to see this through. This time she wasn't going to let him down.

"What is it, exactly, that you want me to believe?"

"In everything you promised. In everything I resisted. We belong together, Logan. You were right all along, even though I was afraid to accept it.

"I'm the one who wasn't giving enough." She hurried on when he closed his eyes and breathed in deeply. "I'm the one who wasn't willing to take the chance. I didn't want to believe in us. In the possibility of us. It scared me because it was so good. Too good to pin any hopes on. Too good to want so badly."

She hesitated, staring hard at the hands she'd clasped tightly together on the table in front of her. "But the past two weeks without you made me see that no matter how afraid I am of fitting into your world, that fear is nothing compared to the reality of not having you in mine."

He looked very weary. "Was it really that difficult to believe in me?"

She shook her head and stalled the threat of tears. "It was belief in myself that posed the problem. Growing up the way I did . . ." She paused, swallowed hard, and began again. "Growing up the way I did, I came to understand certain outcomes were inevitable. I learned to accept less than what I wanted. You don't get hurt when you set your sights low enough. You're never disappointed."

A slow but steady softening relaxed the hard planes of his face. "And you think that's a conclusion exclusive to you?"

"No. It's not exclusive to me." Now came the really tough part. "But where I came from—"

"I know all about where you came from, Carmen," he said, gently cutting her off. "I know everything about you."

Her heart pounded. "You know about my mother?"

"From the beginning. I tried to tell you it never mattered."

"But your father—"

"My father is a sadly selfish man who tries to control other people's lives because he's so dissatisfied with his own."

It was her turn to look away. From the memory of the day Preston Prince had leveled his ultimatum. From the guilt that had been badgering her ever since. "I feel sorry for him," she said quietly. "And I never should have let him intimidate me."

"And I should have warned you he'd try." An anguished look crossed his face. "I still can't believe he gave you money."

"He can't believe I gave it back." A slow smile formed at the memory of her encounter with Preston

Prince just hours before. "The windows are still rattling from his threats."

His answering smile was tentative, tempered with reservations. She intended to dispel every one. "If I had believed in you, he never would have come between us. I'm sorry. I should have let you explain about Juan."

He shrugged. "Preston Prince can be very convincing."

"So can his son—but for all the right reasons that I was too quick to believe were wrong. It's all the power you have, Logan," she added in a bid to make him understand. "It's a difficult thing to see past it to the good it can do, especially when I was feeling so helpless where Juan was concerned."

"I've never wanted you to be anything except what you are."

"I realize that now. And I know that what I was fighting had less to do with our differences than it did with my own doubts. I didn't want to depend on you, but more and more I found that I did.

"I didn't want to let myself love you, but I couldn't stop that either. And against all the odds, I believe you were right when you told me we could make it together. The question is, do you still believe it too?"

She held her breath. Until he held out his hand.

"I believe in us," he whispered, his voice quavering with emotion. "I never stopped. I never want to."

Love swelled inside her breast. Swallowing back tears of relief, she went to him.

"What about Rico?" he asked, pulling her onto his lap.

"He'll cool off."

"And if he doesn't?"

"Then we'll cool him off together. We can handle anything as long as we're together. Even your father," she added, looping her arms around his neck.

"It sounds like you already have." He drew her into his arms and into the kiss they'd both been craving.

When they'd given and taken and reassured themselves that what they were experiencing was real, Logan broke the kiss.

Framing her face in his hands, he pressed his forehead to hers. "This is for keeps, Carmen. I won't let you back away again."

Love, as strong as the heritage she was proud of, as deep as this man's need, made them invincible. "I'm very glad to hear that." She smiled. "I know someone else who will be too. I think Juan's missed you almost as much as I have."

He drew her into another kiss, a kiss that told her how much he'd missed her, and of the hell he'd been through since they'd parted. "I thought I'd lost you. I thought I'd lost you both. And I didn't much like the man I was destined to become without you."

She pulled back and looked deep into his eyes. "Careful. You're talking about the man I fell in love with. And he's not so different from you. Not really. He just needed the right woman to make him see how special he is."

"You fell in love with a beat-up cowboy," he reminded her with that shadow of a grin that never failed to move her.

"That cowboy," she said, cupping his face in her hand, "was my prince disguised as a pauper. And never doubt this Logan—never doubt for an instant that the man I fell in love with was you."

THE EDITOR'S
CORNER

Celebrate the most romantic month of the year with LOVESWEPT! In the six fabulous novels coming your way, you'll thrill to the sexiest heroes and cheer for the most spirited heroines as they discover the power of passion. It's all guaranteed to get you in the mood for love.

Starting the lineup is the ever-popular Fayrene Preston with **STORM SONG**, LOVESWEPT #666— and Noah McKane certainly comes across like a force of nature. He's the hottest act in town, but he never gives interviews, never lets anyone get close to him—until Cate Gallin persuades the powerfully sensual singer to let her capture him on film. Nobody knows the secret they share, the bonds of pain and emotion that go soul-deep . . . or the risks they're taking when Cate accepts the challenge to reveal his stunning talent—without hurting the only man she's ever loved. This compelling novel is proof positive of why Fayrene is one of the best-loved authors of the genre.

SLIGHTLY SHADY by Jan Hudson, LOVE-SWEPT #667, is Maggie Marino's first impression of the brooding desperado she sees in the run-down bar. On the run from powerful forces, she's gotten stranded deep in the heart of Texas, and the last thing she wants is to tangle with a mesmerizing outlaw who calls himself Shade. But Shade knows just how to comfort a woman, and Maggie soon finds herself surrendering to his sizzling looks—even as she wonders what secret he's hiding. To tantalize you even further, we'll tell you that Shade is truly Paul Berringer, a tiger of the business world and brother of the Berringer twins who captivated you in **BIG AND BRIGHT** and **CALL ME SIN**. So don't miss out on Paul's own story. Bad boys don't come any better, and as usual Jan Hudson's writing shines with humor and sizzles with sensuality.

Please give a warm welcome to Gayle Kasper and her very first LOVESWEPT, **TENDER, LOVING CURE**, #668. As you may have guessed, this utterly delightful romance features a doctor, and there isn't a finer one than Joel Benedict. He'd do anything to become even better—except attend a sex talk seminar. He changes his mind, though, when he catches a glimpse of the teacher. Maggie Springer is a temptress who makes Joel think of private lessons, and when a taste of her kissable lips sparks the fire beneath his cool facade, he starts to believe that it's possible for him to love once more. We're happy to be Gayle's publisher, and this terrific novel will show you why.

Sally Goldenbaum returns to LOVESWEPT with **MOONLIGHT ON MONTEREY BAY**, #669. The beach in that part of California has always been special to Sam Eastland, and when he goes to his empty house there, he doesn't expect to discover a beautiful nymph. Interior decorator Maddie Ames fights to convince him that only she can create a sanctuary to soothe his troubled spirit . . . and he's too spellbound to refuse. But when their attraction flares into burning passion and Sam fears he can't give Maddie the joy she deserves, she must persuade him not to underestimate the power of love. Vibrant with heartfelt emotion, this romance showcases Sally's evocative writing. Welcome back, Sally!

A spooky manor house, things that go bump in the night—all this and more await you in **MIDNIGHT LADY**, LOVESWEPT #670, by Linda Wisdom. The granddaughter of the king of horror movies, Samantha Lyons knows all about scare tactics, and she uses them to try to keep Kyle Fletcher from getting the inside scoop about her family's film studio. But the devastatingly handsome reporter isn't about to abandon the story—or break the sensual magic that has woven itself around him and beautiful Sam . . . even if wooing her means facing down ghosts! Hold on to your seats because Linda is about to take you on a roller-coaster ride of dangerous desires and exquisite sensations.

It **LOOKS LIKE LOVE** when Drew Webster first sees Jill Stuart in Susan Connell's new LOVESWEPT, #671. Jill is a delicious early-morning surprise, clad in silky lingerie, kneeling in Drew's uncle's yard, and coaxing a puppy into her arms. Drew knows instantly that she wouldn't have to beg him to come running, and he sets off on a passionate courtship. To Jill, temptation has never looked or felt so good, but when Drew insists that there's a thief in the retirement community she manages, she tells him it can't be true, that she has everything under control. Drew wants to trust her, but can he believe the angel who's stolen his heart?

Susan delivers a wonderful love story that will warm your heart.

Happy reading!

With warmest wishes,

Nita Taublib

Nita Taublib
Associate Publisher

P.S. Don't miss the exciting women's novels from Bantam that are coming your way in February—**THE BELOVED SCOUNDREL** by nationally bestselling author Iris Johansen, a tempestuous tale of abduction, seduction, and surrender that sweeps from the shimmering halls of Regency England to the decadent haunts of a notorious rogue; **VIXEN** by award-winning author Jane Feather, a spectacular historical romance in which an iron-willed nobleman suddenly becomes the guardian of a mischievous, orphaned beauty; and **ONE FINE DAY** by supertalented Theresa Weir, which tells the searing story of a second chance for happiness for Molly and Austin Bennet, two memorable characters from Theresa's previous novel **FOREVER**. We'll be giving you a sneak peek at these terrific books in next month's LOVESWEPTs. And immediately following this page look for a preview of the exciting romances from Bantam that are *available now!*

Don't miss these exciting books by your
favorite Bantam authors

On sale in December:

DESIRE
by Amanda Quick

LONG TIME COMING
by Sandra Brown

STRANGER IN MY ARMS
by R.J. Kaiser

WHERE DOLPHINS GO
by Peggy Webb

And in hardcover from Doubleday
AMAZON LILY
by Theresa Weir

Amanda Quick

New York Times bestselling author of
DANGEROUS and **DECEPTION**

DESIRE

This spectacular novel is Amanda Quick's first medieval romance!

*From the windswept, craggy coast of a remote British isle comes
the thrilling tale of a daring lady and a dangerous knight who are
bound by the tempests of fate and by the dawning of desire . . .*

"There was something you wished to discuss with me, sir?"

"Aye. Our marriage."

Clare flinched, but she did not fall off the bench. Under
the circumstances, she considered that a great accomplishment. "You are very direct about matters, sir."

He looked mildly surprised. "I see no point in being
otherwise."

"Nor do I. Very well, sir, let me be blunt. In spite of
your efforts to establish yourself in everyone's eyes as the
sole suitor for my hand, I must tell you again that your
expectations are unrealistic."

"Nay, madam," Gareth said very quietly. "'Tis your
expectations that are unrealistic. I read the letter you sent
to Lord Thurston. It is obvious you hope to marry a phantom, a man who does not exist. I fear you must settle for
something less than perfection."

She lifted her chin. "You think that no man can be found who suits my requirements?"

"I believe that we are both old enough and wise enough to know that marriage is a practical matter. It has nothing to do with the passions that the troubadours make so much of in their foolish ballads."

Clare clasped her hands together very tightly. "Kindly do not condescend to lecture me on the subject of marriage, sir. I am only too well aware that in my case it is a matter of duty, not desire. But in truth, when I composed my recipe for a husband, I did not believe that I was asking for so very much."

"Mayhap you will discover enough good points in me to satisfy you, madam."

Clare blinked. "Do you actually believe that?"

"I would ask you to examine closely what I have to offer. I think that I can meet a goodly portion of your requirements."

She surveyed him from head to toe. "You most definitely do not meet my requirements in the matter of size."

"Concerning my size, as I said earlier, there is little I can do about it, but I assure you I do not generally rely upon it to obtain my ends."

Clare gave a ladylike snort of disbelief.

"'Tis true. I prefer to use my wits rather than muscle whenever possible."

"Sir, I shall be frank. I want a man of peace for this isle. Desire has never known violence. I intend to keep things that way. I do not want a husband who thrives on the sport of war."

He looked down at her with an expression of surprise. "I have no love of violence or war."

Clare raised her brows. "Are you going to tell me that you have no interest in either? You, who carry a sword with a terrible name? You, who wear a reputation as a destroyer of murderers and thieves?"

"I did not say I had no interest in such matters. I have, after all, used a warrior's skills to make my way in the world. They are the tools of my trade, that's all."

"A fine point, sir."

"But a valid one. I have grown weary of violence, madam. I seek a quiet, peaceful life."

Clare did not bother to hide her skepticism. "An interesting statement, given your choice of career."

"I did not have much choice in the matter of my career," Gareth said. "Did you?"

"Nay, but that is—"

"Let us go on to your second requirement. You wrote that you desire a man of cheerful countenance and even temperament."

She stared at him, astonished. "You consider yourself a man of cheerful countenance?"

"Nay, I admit that I have been told my countenance is somewhat less than cheerful. But I am most definitely a man of even temperament."

"I do not believe that for a moment, sir."

"I promise you, it is the truth. You may inquire of anyone who knows me. Ask Sir Ulrich. He has been my companion for years. He will tell you that I am the most even-tempered of men. I am not given to fits of rage or foul temper."

Or to mirth and laughter, either, Clare thought as she met his smoky crystal eyes. "Very well, I shall grant that you may be even-tempered in a certain sense, although that was not quite what I had in mind."

"You see? We are making progress here." Gareth reached up to grasp a limb of the apple tree. "Now, then, to continue. Regarding your last requirement, I remind you yet again that I can read."

Clare cast about frantically for a fresh tactic. "Enough, sir. I grant that you meet a small number of my requirements if one interprets them very broadly. But what about our own? Surely there are some specific things you seek in a wife."

"My requirements?" Gareth looked taken back by the question. "My requirements in a wife are simple, madam. I believe that you will satisfy them."

"Because I hold lands and the recipes of a plump perfume business? Think twice before you decide that is sufficient to satisfy you sir. We live a simple life here on Desire. Quite boring in most respects. You are a man who is no doubt accustomed to the grand entertainments provided in the households of great lords."

"I can do without such entertainments, my lady. They hold no appeal for me."

"You have obviously lived an adventurous, exciting life," Clare persisted. "Will you find contentment in the business of growing flowers and making perfumes?"

"Aye, madam, I will," Gareth said with soft satisfaction.

"'Tis hardly a career suited to a knight of your reputation, sir."

"Rest assured that here on Desire I expect to find the things that are most important to me."

Clare lost patience with his reasonableness. "And just what are those things, sir?"

"Lands, a hall of my own, and a woman who can give me a family." Gareth reached down and pulled her to her feet as effortlessly as though she were fashioned of thistledown. "You can provide me with all of those things, lady. That makes you very valuable to me. Do not imagine that I will not protect you well. And do not think that I will let you slip out of my grasp."

"But—"

Gareth brought his mouth down on hers, silencing her protest.

LONG TIME COMING
by

SANDRA BROWN

Blockbuster author Sandra Brown—whose name is almost synonymous with the *New York Times* bestseller list—offers up a classic romantic novel that aches with emotion and sizzles with passion . . .

For sixteen years Marnie Hibbs had raised her sister's son as her own, hoping that her love would make up for the father David would never know . . . dreaming that someday David's father would find his way back into her life. And then one afternoon Marnie looked up and Law Kincaid was there, as strong and heartbreakingly handsome as ever. Flooded with bittersweet memories, Marnie yearned to lose herself in his arms, yet a desperate fear held her back, for this glorious man who had given her David now had the power to take him away. . . .

The Porsche crept along the street like a sleek black panther. Hugging the curb, its engine purred so deep and low it sounded like a predator's growl.

Marnie Hibbs was kneeling in the fertile soil of her flower bed, digging among the impatiens under the ligustrum bushes and cursing the little bugs that made three meals a day of them, when the sound of the car's motor attracted her attention. She glanced at it over her shoulder, then panicked as it came to a stop in front of her house.

"Lord, is it that late?" she muttered. Dropping her trowel, she stood up and brushed the clinging damp earth off her bare knees.

She reached up to push her dark bangs off her forehead before she realized that she still had on her heavy gardening gloves. Quickly she peeled them off and dropped them beside the trowel, all the while watching the driver get out of the sports car and start up her front walk.

Glancing at her wristwatch, she saw that she hadn't lost track of time. He was just very early for their appointment, and as a result, she wasn't going to make a very good first impression. Being hot, sweaty, and dirty was no way to meet a client. And she needed this commission badly.

Forcing a smile, she moved down the sidewalk to greet him, nervously trying to remember if she had left the house and studio reasonably neat when she decided to do an hour's worth of yard work. She had planned to tidy up before he arrived.

She might look like the devil, but she didn't want to appear intimidated. Self-confident friendliness was the only way to combat the disadvantage of having been caught looking her worst.

He was still several yards away from her when she greeted him. "Hello," she said with a bright smile. "Obviously we got our signals switched. I thought you weren't coming until later."

"I decided this diabolical game of yours had gone on long enough."

Marnie's sneakers skidded on the old concrete walk as she came to an abrupt halt. She tilted her head in stunned surprise. "I'm sorry, I—"

"Who the hell are you, lady?"

"Miss Hibbs. Who do you think?"

"Never heard of you. Just what the devil are you up to?"

"Up to?" She glanced around helplessly, as though the giant sycamores in her front yard might provide an answer to this bizarre interrogation.

"Why've you been sending me those letters?"

"Letters?"

He was clearly furious, and her lack of comprehension only seemed to make him angrier. He bore down on her like a hawk on a field mouse, until she had to bow her back to look up at him. The summer sun was behind him, casting him in silhouette.

He was blond, tall, trim, and dressed in casual slacks and a sport shirt—all stylish, impeccably so. He was wearing opaque aviator glasses, so she couldn't see his eyes, but if they were as belligerent as his expression and stance, she was better off not seeing them.

"I don't know what you're talking about."

"The letters, lady, the letters." He strained the words through a set of strong white teeth.

"*What* letters?"

"Don't play dumb."

"Are you sure you've got the right house?"

He took another step forward. "I've got the right house," he said in a voice that was little more than a snarl.

"Obviously you don't." She didn't like being put on the defensive, especially by someone she'd never met over something of which she was totally ignorant. "You're either crazy or drunk, but in any case, you're *wrong*. I'm not the person you're looking for and I demand that you leave my property. Now."

"You were expecting me. I could tell by the way you spoke to me."

"I thought you were the man from the advertising agency."

"Well, I'm not."

"Thank God." She would hate having to do business with someone this irrational and ill-tempered.

"You know damn well who I am," he said, peeling off the sunglasses.

Marnie sucked in a quick, sharp breath and fell back a step because she did indeed know who he was. She raised a hand to her chest in an attempt at keeping her jumping heart in place. "Law," she gasped.

"That's right. Law Kincaid. Just like you wrote it on the envelopes."

She was shocked to see him after all these years, standing only inches in front of her. This time he wasn't merely a familiar image in the newspaper or on her television screen. He was flesh and blood. The years had been kind to that flesh, improving his looks, not eroding them.

She wanted to stand and stare, but he was staring at her with unmitigated contempt and no recognition at all. "Let's go inside, Mr. Kincaid," she suggested softly.

STRANGER IN MY ARMS
by
R.J. KAISER

With the chilling tension of Hitchcock and the passionate heat of Sandra Brown, STRANGER IN MY ARMS is a riveting novel of romantic suspense in which a woman with amnesia suspects she is a target for murder.

Here is a look at this powerful novel . . .

"Tell me who you are, Carter, where you came from, about your past—everything."

He complied, giving me a modest summary of his life. He'd started his career in New York and formed a partnership with a British firm in London. When his partners suffered financial difficulties, he convinced my father to buy them out. Altogether he'd been in Europe for twelve years.

Carter was forty, ten years older than I. He'd been born and raised in Virginia, where his parents still resided. He'd attended Dartmouth and the Harvard Business School. In addition to the villa he had a house in Kensington, a flat off the avenue Bosquet in Paris, and a small farm outside Charlottesville, Virginia.

After completing his discourse, he leaned back and sipped his coffee. I watched him while Yvonne cleared the table.

Carter Bass was an attractive man with sophistication and class. He was well-spoken, educated. But mainly he appealed to me because I felt a connection with him, tortured though it was. We'd been dancing around each other since he'd appeared on the scene, our history at war with our more immediate and intangible feelings toward each other.

I could only assume that the allure he held for me had to do with the fact that he was both a stranger and my husband. My body, in effect, remembered Carter as my mind could not.

I picked up my coffee cup, but paused with it at my lips. Something had been troubling me for some time and I decided to blurt it out. "Do you have a mistress, Carter?"

He blinked. "What kind of a question is that?"

"A serious one. You know all about me, it's only fair I know about you."

"I don't have a mistress."

"Are you lonely?"

He smiled indulgently. "Hillary, we have an unspoken agreement. You don't ask and neither do I."

"Then you don't want to talk about it? I should mind my own business, is that what you mean?"

He contemplated me. "Maybe we should step out onto the terrace for some air—sort of clear our mental palate."

"If you like."

Carter came round and helped me up. "Could I interest you in a brandy?"

"I don't think so. I enjoyed the wine. That's really all I'd like."

He took my arm and we went through the salon and onto the terrace. He kept his hand on my elbow, though I was no longer shaky. His attention was flattering, and I decided I liked the changing chemistry between us, even though I had so many doubts.

It was a clear night and there were countless stars. I inhaled the pleasantly cool air and looked at my husband. Carter let his hand drop away.

"I miss this place," he said.

"Did I drive you away?"

"No, I've stayed away by choice."

"It's all so sad," I said, staring off down the dark valley. "I think we're a tragic pair. People shouldn't be as unhappy as we seem to be."

"You're talking about the past. Amnesiacs aren't supposed to do that, my dear."

I smiled at his teasing.

"I'm learning all about myself, about us, very quickly."

"I wonder if you're better off not knowing," he said, a trace of sadness in his voice.

"I can't run away from who I am," I replied.

"No, I suppose you can't."

"You'd like for me to change, though, wouldn't you?"

"What difference does it make? Your condition is temporary. It's probably better in the long run to treat you as the person I know you to be."

His words seemed cruel—or at least unkind—though what he was saying was not only obvious, it was also reasonable. Why should he assume the burden of my sins? I sighed and looked away.

"I'd like to believe in you, Hillary," he said. "But it isn't as simple as just giving you the benefit of the doubt."

"If I could erase the past, I would." My eyes shimmered. "But even if you were willing, *they* wouldn't let me."

Carter knew whom I was referring to. "They" were the police, and "they" were coming for me in the morning, though their purpose was still somewhat vague. "They" were the whole issue, it seemed to me—maybe the final arbiter of who I really was. My past not only defined me, it was my destiny.

"I don't think you should jump to any conclusions," he said. "Let's wait and see what they have to say."

He reached out and took my bare arms, seemingly to savor the feel of my skin. His hands were quite warm, and he gripped me firmly as he searched my eyes. I was sure then that he had brought me to the terrace to touch me, to connect with me physically. He had wanted to be close to me. And maybe I'd come along because I wanted to be close to him.

There were signs of desire in Carter's eyes. Heat. My heart picked up its beat when he lowered his mouth toward mine. His kiss was tender and it aroused me. I'd hungered for this—for the affirmation, for the affection—more than I knew. But still I wasn't prepared for it. I didn't expect to want him as much as I did.

I kissed Carter every bit as deeply as he kissed me. Then, at exactly the same moment, we pulled apart, retreating as swiftly as we'd come together. When I looked into his eyes I saw the reflection of my own feelings—the same doubt, distrust, and fear that I myself felt.

And when he released me, I realized that the issues separating us remained unresolved. The past, like the future, was undeniable. The morning would come. It would come much too soon.

WHERE DOLPHINS GO
by
PEGGY WEBB

"Ms. Webb has an inventive mind brimming
with originality that makes all of her books
special reading."
—*Romantic Times*

*To Susan Riley, the dolphins at the Oceanfront Research Center
were her last chance to reach her frail, broken child. Yet when she
brought Jeffy to the Center, she never expected to have to contend
with a prickly doctor who made it clear that he didn't intend to
get involved. Quiet, handsome, and hostile, Paul Taylor was a
wounded man, and when Susan learned of the tragedy behind his
anguish, she knew she had to help. But what began as compassion
soon turned to desire, and now Susan was falling for a man who
belonged to someone else. . . .*

"A woman came to see me today," Bill said. "A woman and
a little boy."

Paul went very still.

"Her name is Susan . . . Susan Riley. She knew about the
center from that article in the newspaper last week."

There had been many articles written about Dr. Bill
McKenzie and the research he did with dolphins. The most
recent one, though, had delved into the personality of the
dolphins themselves. An enterprising reporter had done his
homework. "Dolphins," he had written, "relate well to people. Some even seem to have extrasensory perception. They
seem to sense when a person is sick or hurt or depressed."

"Her little boy has a condition called truncus arteriosus . . ." Bill squinted in the way he always did when he
was judging a person's reaction.

Paul was careful not to show one. *Truncus arteriosus. A condition of the heart. Malfunctioning arteries. Surgery required.*

"Bill, I don't practice medicine anymore."

"I'm not asking you to practice medicine. I'm asking you to listen."

"I'm listening."

"The boy was scheduled for surgery, but he had a stroke before it could be performed."

For God's sake, Paul. Do something. DO SOMETHING!

"Bill . . ."

"The child is depressed, doesn't respond to anything, anybody. She thought the dolphins might be the answer. She wanted to bring him here on a regular basis."

"You told her no, of course."

"I'm a marine biologist, not a psychologist." Bill slumped in his chair. "I told her no."

"The child needs therapy, not dolphins."

"That's what I thought, but now . . ." Bill gave Paul that squinty-eyed look. "You're a doctor, Paul. Maybe if I let her bring the boy here during feeding times—"

"No. Dammit, Bill. Look at me. I can't even help myself, let alone a dying child and a desperate mother."

Bill looked down at his shoes and counted to ten under his breath. When he looked up Paul could see the pity in his eyes.

He hated that most of all. . . .

Susan hadn't meant to cry.

She knew before she came to the Oceanfront Research Center that her chances of success were slim. And yet she had to try. She couldn't live with herself if she didn't do everything in her power to help Jeffy.

Her face was already wet with tears as she lifted her child from his stroller and placed him in the car. He was so lifeless, almost as if he had already died and had forgotten to take his body with him. When she bent over him to fasten the seat belt, her tears dripped onto his still face.

He didn't even notice.

She swiped at her tears, mad at herself. Crying wasn't going to help Jeffy. Crying wasn't going to help either of them.

Resolutely she folded the stroller and put it in the backseat. Then she blew her nose and climbed into the driver's seat. Couldn't let Jeffy know she was sad. Did he see? Did he know?

The doctors had assured her that he did. That the stroke damage had been confined to areas of the brain that affected his motor control. That his bright little mind and his personality were untouched. And yet, he sat beside her like some discarded rag doll, staring at nothing.

Fighting hard against the helpless feeling she sometimes got when she looked at Jeffy, she turned the key in the ignition and waited for the old engine to warm up. She was not helpless. And she refused to let herself become that way.

"Remember that little song you love so much, Jeffy? The one Mommy wrote?" Jeffy stared at his small sneakers.

Sweat plastered Susan's hair to the sides of her face and made the back of her sundress stick to the seat.

"Mommy's going to sing it to you, darling, while we drive." She put the car into gear and backed out of the parking space, giving herself time to get the quiver out of her voice. She was *not* going to cry again. "You remember the words, don't you, sweetheart? Help Mommy sing, Jeffy."

" 'Sing with a voice of gladness; sing with a voice of joy.' " Susan's voice was neither glad nor joyful, but at least it no longer quivered. Control was easier in the daytime. It was at night, lying in the dark all by herself, when she lost it. She had cried herself to sleep many nights, muffling the sounds in the pillow in case Jeffy, sleeping in the next room, could hear.

" 'Shout for the times of goodness.' " How many good times could Jeffy remember? " 'Shout for the time of cheer.' " How many happy times had he had? Born with a heart condition, he had missed the ordinary joys other children took for granted—chasing a dog, kicking a ball, tumbling in the leaves, outrunning the wind.

" 'Sing with a voice that's hopeful . . . ' " Susan sang on, determined to be brave, determined to bring her child back from that dark, silent world he had entered.

As the car took a curve, Jeffy's head lolled to the side so he was staring straight at her. All the brightness of childhood that should be in his eyes was dulled over by four years of pain and defeat.

Why do you let me hurt?

The message in those eyes made her heart break.

The song died on her lips, the last clear notes lingering in the car like a party guest who didn't know it was time to go home. Susan turned her head to look out the window.

Biloxi was parching under the late afternoon sun. Dust devils shimmered in the streets. Palm trees, sagging and dusty, looked as tired as she felt. It seemed years since she had had a peaceful night's sleep. An eternity since she had had a day of fun and relaxation.

She was selfish to the core. Thinking about her own needs, her own desires. She had to think about Jeffy. There must be something that would spark his interest besides the dolphins.

And don't miss these heart-stopping
romances from Bantam Books,
on sale in January

THE BELOVED SCOUNDREL
by the nationally bestselling author
Iris Johansen
"You'll be riveted from beginning to end
as [Iris Johansen] holds you captive to a
love story of grand proportions."
—*Romantic Times* on
The Magnificent Rogue

VIXEN
by **Jane Feather**
A passionate tale of an iron-willed
nobleman who suddenly becomes the
guardian of a mischievous, orphaned
beauty.

ONE FINE DAY
by **Theresa Weir**
"Theresa Weir's writing is poignant,
passionate and powerful. *One Fine Day*
delivers intense emotion and compelling
characters that will capture the
hearts of readers."
—*New York Times* bestselling
author Jayne Ann Krentz

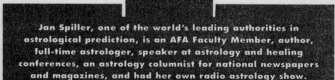

OFFICIAL RULES

To enter the sweepstakes below carefully follow all instructions found elsewhere in this offer.

The **Winners Classic** will award prizes with the following approximate maximum values: 1 Grand Prize: $26,500 (or $25,000 cash alternate); 1 First Prize: $3,000; 5 Second Prizes: $400 each; 35 Third Prizes: $100 each; 1,000 Fourth Prizes: $7.50 each. Total maximum retail value of Winners Classic Sweepstakes is $42,500. Some presentations of this sweepstakes may contain individual entry numbers corresponding to one or more of the aforementioned prize levels. To determine the Winners, individual entry numbers will first be compared with the winning numbers preselected by computer. For winning numbers not returned, prizes will be awarded in random drawings from among all eligible entries received. Prize choices may be offered at various levels. If a winner chooses an automobile prize, all license and registration fees, taxes, destination charges and, other expenses not offered herein are the responsibility of the winner. If a winner chooses a trip, travel must be complete within one year from the time the prize is awarded. Minors must be accompanied by an adult. Travel companion(s) must also sign release of liability. Trips are subject to space and departure availability. Certain black-out dates may apply.

The following applies to the sweepstakes named above:

No purchase necessary. You can also enter the sweepstakes by sending your name and address to: P.O. Box 508, Gibbstown, N.J. 08027. Mail each entry separately. Sweepstakes begins 6/1/93. Entries must be received by 12/30/94. Not responsible for lost, late, damaged, misdirected, illegible or postage due mail. Mechanically reproduced entries are not eligible. All entries become property of the sponsor and will not be returned.

Prize Selection/Validations: Selection of winners will be conducted no later than 5:00 PM on January 28, 1995, by an independent judging organization whose decisions are final. Random drawings will be held at 1211 Avenue of the Americas, New York, N.Y. 10036. Entrants need not be present to win. Odds of winning are determined by total number of entries received. Circulation of this sweepstakes is estimated not to exceed 200 million. All prizes are guaranteed to be awarded and delivered to winners. Winners will be notified by mail and may be required to complete an affidavit of eligibility and release of liability which must be returned within 14 days of date on notification or alternate winners will be selected in a random drawing. Any prize notification letter or any prize returned to a participating sponsor, Bantam Doubleday Dell Publishing Group, Inc., its participating divisions or subsidiaries, or the independent judging organization as undeliverable will be awarded to an alternate winner. Prizes are not transferable. No substitution for prizes except as offered or as may be necessary due to unavailability, in which case a prize of equal or greater value will be awarded. Prizes will be awarded approximately 90 days after the drawing. All taxes are the sole responsibility of the winners. Entry constitutes permission (except where prohibited by law) to use winners' names, hometowns, and likenesses for publicity purposes without further or other compensation. Prizes won by minors will be awarded in the name of parent or legal guardian.

Participation: Sweepstakes open to residents of the United States and Canada, except for the province of Quebec. Sweepstakes sponsored by Bantam Doubleday Dell Publishing Group, Inc., (BDD), 1540 Broadway, New York, NY 10036. Versions of this sweepstakes with different graphics and prize choices will be offered in conjunction with various solicitations or promotions by different subsidiaries and divisions of BDD. Where applicable, winners will have their choice of any prize offered at level won. Employees of BDD, its divisions, subsidiaries, advertising agencies, independent judging organization, and their immediate family members are not eligible.

Canadian residents, in order to win, must first correctly answer a time limited arithmetical skill testing question. Void in Puerto Rico, Quebec and wherever prohibited or restricted by law. Subject to all federal, state, local and provincial laws and regulations. For a list of major prize winners (available after 1/29/95): send a self-addressed, stamped envelope entirely separate from your entry to: Sweepstakes Winners, P.O. Box 517, Gibbstown, NJ 08027. Requests must be received by 12/30/94. DO NOT SEND ANY OTHER CORRESPONDENCE TO THIS P.O. BOX.